Knowing everything she had
been through, Alex wanted her to relax
over a garden. Grin at his kids. Make his
daughter's perpetual frown disappear.

He hiked a brow. "Dinner at six?"

She started to say something, then caught
herself and shook her head. "Not a good idea."

Alex stayed low-key and stretched out his
single-word question. "Because?"

"You have issues with my issues. I have issues
with my issues. End of story."

She almost shouted the last comment, and that
made him smile. "Good cops learn to deal with
issues. And you need to eat."

"I'm thirty-three years old, I've been feeding
myself for a while, but thanks anyway.
However, I would love to do Emma's project.
That's it."

Alex feigned acceptance. The best investigators
knew to plant seeds of doubt, guilt or need...
then walk away, hoping evidence would come
to them.

With Lisa, he was willing to wait.

Books by Ruth Logan Herne

Love Inspired

RUTH LOGAN HERNE

Born into poverty, Ruth puts great stock in one of her favorite Ben Franklinisms: "Having been poor is no shame. Being ashamed of it is." With God-given appreciation for the amazing opportunities abounding in our land, Ruth finds simple gifts in the everyday blessings of smudge-faced small children, bright flowers, freshly baked goods, good friends, family, puppies and higher education. She believes a good woman should never fear dirt, snakes or spiders, all of which like to infest her aged farmhouse, necessitating a good pair of tongs for extracting the snakes, a flat-bottomed shoe for the spiders, and for the dirt…

Simply put, she's learned that some things aren't worth fretting about! If you laugh in the face of dust and love to talk about God, men, romance, great shoes and wonderful food, feel free to contact Ruth through her website at www.ruthloganherne.com.

The Lawman's Second Chance

Ruth Logan Herne

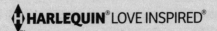

Recycling programs
for this product may
not exist in your area.

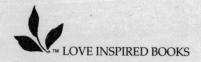

™ LOVE INSPIRED BOOKS

ISBN-13: 978-0-373-81692-7

THE LAWMAN'S SECOND CHANCE

www.LoveInspiredBooks.com

Printed in U.S.A.

Do not fear, for I am with you. Do not be afraid, for I am your God; I will strengthen you, I will help you, I will uphold you with my victorious right hand.
—*Isaiah* 41:10

For Lisa Wehrfritz Tydings and Beth Endlich, one here, one in heaven. Your battles inspired both sides of this tender story. May God bless you and keep you in his loving embrace, always.

Acknowledgments

First and foremost I have to thank my beautiful friend Lisa Wehrfritz Tydings. Girlfriend, you went to extremes to get me firsthand info…. Next time we'll limit our research to books, okay? To Jeff Tydings for his candor and humor and amazing belief in God. You set the bar high for any man dealing with a life-threatening illness while surrounded by four kids under eleven. You rock. To Taylor, McKenna, Nolan and Brody Tydings, the four children I've cared for since their births. I love each and every one of you, which is why I like to torture you… It's what I *do*. Huge thanks to Lisa and Jeff's families for allowing us to be part of their help brigade. Devoted thanks to Love Inspired Senior Editor Melissa Endlich, who encouraged my work on this book. Her warmth and wisdom helped strengthen these pages from beginning to end. The dedication tribute to her mother, Beth Endlich, is heartfelt and sincere. Regardless of circumstances, we are never ready to kiss our mothers goodbye.

Heartfelt thanks to Van Putte Gardens in Greece, whose Breast Cancer Awareness Pink Flower Campaign inspired the fictional "Lisa's" campaign. I walked into their garden center just days after the real Lisa's diagnosis and knew God put me there, surrounding me with pink, filling me with hope.

To the Hilton community, the Hilton Central School district, St. Leo the Great Catholic Church, Lisa's coworkers, fellow parishioners, neighbors and friends who stocked refrigerators, drove kids and prayed unceasingly. You are wonderful people. Your help will never be forgotten. And last but never least to our amazing day-care moms surrounding Lisa, who fearlessly took up the cause to help when one of their own was threatened. The Pink Garden, the Fight-Like-A-Girl party, the T-shirts, the videos… the constant love and support (and yes, even the tears…). Lisa couldn't be embraced by a more loving, caring, devoted group of women and I bless our time together, every single day.

Chapter One

Lieutenant Alexander Steele turned into the parking lot of Gardens & Greens Nursery and pulled up short. Shades of pink surrounded him while huge banners proclaimed the garden center's tribute to breast cancer awareness.

The Southern Tier investigator had three choices. Fight the bile rising in his throat, drive the car away and disappoint his ten-year-old daughter yet again, or man up and choose a parking spot.

He chose the latter and pretended to like it, but he'd been pretending for too long and the garden center's Pink Ribbon Campaign slam-dunked his already damaged heart. Why here? Why now? He'd made the move to Allegany County not only to get away from the city, but also to escape the grief breast cancer had left behind.

Realization hit home. Spring had arrived, finally.

May loomed just around the corner. That meant Mother's Day.

Of course. He hadn't thought of that. Was it a deliberate mistake, like so many others of late? Or was he simply bogged down with work and the task of raising three motherless kids?

"Oh, Daddy." Emma's gray eyes rounded as she grasped his hand. "Have you ever seen anything so beautiful in your life?"

The crush of pinks wasn't beautiful. Not to him. Not when every ribbon, every banner, every rose-toned bloom and 5K run reminded him of what he'd lost two years before. His wife. His helpmate, appointed by God.

He'd believed that then.

He believed it now. So pardon him while he internally recoiled at memories of the killer disease that robbed Jenny of her life and him of the wife he'd had for too short a time.

"I...um..."

She looked up at him. Met his gaze. Her little hand clasped his in solidarity beyond childlike understanding. "I miss her every time I see pink flowers."

The bile rose further. Or maybe it was just a lump in his throat, inspired by Emma's unshed tears. But she recovered faster than he did, and tugged him forward. "We need to see what they have, find Miss Fitzgerald, then do a sketch."

"A sketch?" The look she angled his way said he hadn't been listening. Guilty as charged. "What sketch?"

"Of the yard, Dad." She pressed her lips together, and pulled him to the right. "Let's start over here."

More pink. Great.

A teenager paused in front of them and offered a tray of sugar cookies. Cookies done in the shape of a breast cancer ribbon. Pale pink frosting outlined the loop and a dusting of rose and white sprinkles sparkled in the late morning sun. Emma accepted one with a bright smile.

Alex would rather choke down potting soil than eat one of those cookies. He shook his head, hoping his expression didn't reflect the darkness in his heart.

Who in their right mind expected this many shades of pink? Not him. And he didn't like it at all.

"What are these, Dad?" Emma lingered, her notebook in hand. She took out his digital camera and snapped a pic of the pink flowering bush. "I like them. A lot."

Of course she would. They were pink and Emma was a girl. One plus one equaled… "The ticket says it's a Sugar Plum hydrangea."

"So pretty." Emma copied the name into her notebook and studied the card. "Some sun, light shade, keep moist. Which side of our house is best for that?"

They'd bought a historic village home over the winter, a house far removed from the modern center split he and Jenny shared for twelve short years of marriage on the east side of Rochester.

He'd needed *different,* a new setting. He actively sought change in every way he could—house, job and location.

He did manage to keep the same three children, mostly because they were too noisy to bring much on the black market. Or maybe because he could keep them safer here in this sweet, pastoral town.

Down here, in the rolling hills of Allegany and Cattaraugus Counties, he could leave the drug-riddled city streets behind him. A new start, personally and professionally. Safer for his heart, better for his soul. He'd had enough of gang warfare, racketeering and neglected children to last a lifetime. He'd faced every kind of evil known to man, and he'd won the day sometimes.

But not always.

Jenny's death meant it was time to leave. Seek anew. Begin again.

He'd gotten the two older kids settled into Jamison Elementary School, Emma in fourth grade and Becky in second. Little Joshua went to a preschool facility. The day school was pricey but the hours worked well with Alex's demanding schedule. Saving Jenny's life insurance money for Josh's college education would be redundant if the kid flunked kindergarten.

Jenny had possessed a knack for teaching little ones, as if life's lessons were intrinsic to her personality. His knack was for solving crime. Directing a troop of officers. And playing with kids. They'd made a great team.

And then she died.

His heart seized again, the garden store celebration a kick in the head to a widower barely getting by.

"You look lost."

Alex turned and faced a pair of the prettiest brown eyes he'd ever seen. Dark. Bright. Engaging. Filled with humor. "Do we?"

She nodded and bent to Emma's level, the midspring sun sparkling soft rays of light from her dark, wavy hair. "Well. He does." She jerked a thumb his way, and the way she did it, as if she and Em were simpatico and in league against him, made him smile.

"He is," Emma agreed. "Actually, we both are, Miss…?"

"Lisa." The woman stuck out a hand to Emma, shook hers, then stood again. "Lisa Fitzgerald. And you are?"

"Alex." He accepted the handshake and the smile, and for just a moment felt like he'd been transported into a world of warmth again. Kindness. Gentleness. And it felt good. "Alex Steele. And my daughter, Emma."

Recognition deepened Lisa's smile. "From the

4-H club. I got an email saying you'd be contacting me." She encompassed both of them with her question and expression. "So what have we got going, Alex and Emma? This can seem a little overwhelming when you first arrive."

And then some, thought Alex, but not the way she meant. The vast variety of plants and gardening products covered acres of land. Two sprawling red barns stood along the far side, and a newer building, a retail-store Morton building, linked to the nearest barn. Distant greenhouses stretched north and south in tidy rows of plastic-wrapped metal tubing while closer hothouses lined the brick walk. They were filled with wide rows of potted flowers under blooming hanging baskets done in various shades of pink and rose.

Right now he hated pink with an intensity that rivaled his aversion for cooked spinach, and he'd never hated anything as much as cooked spinach.

"I'm doing a kind of massive project," Emma explained. "And my leader said I should come here and see you first. To see if you could be my adviser."

Lisa didn't look surprised. "That's because my mother was a 4-H leader and worked on all kinds of projects, from raising calves to starting seedlings. I've taken on a tiny bit of what she used to do. And I do believe Mrs. Reddenbach's email used the words 'precociously bright.'" She bent low. "I'm not all that good with cows, so please tell me you're here about gardening tips. As long as it's about plants and dirt, I'm your go-to person." Her wistful face implored the girl to avoid all questions relating to farm animals.

Emma nodded, delighted. "Just gardens. At our house. If you can help us."

"Phew!" Lisa swept a hand across her smooth brow.

Alex relaxed a little more. Maybe this woman could guide them through the intricacies of planning and implementing a garden. It had seemed easy enough when Emma approached him after her first 4-H meeting, but then he realized a garden, in overachiever Emma's mind, meant the entire circumference of their home and would take months to complete.

Oops.

But it was the first thing she'd shown strong interest in since Jenny's death, and he couldn't deny her a chance to heal. To move on. To embrace life.

You could try taking your own advice. Start living in the here and now.

He ignored the internal ruminations. With three kids and a full-time job, an eight-room house and a yard in dire need of attention, he had enough on his plate. He'd save the psychobabble for some day when he had time to breathe again.

"What kind of garden are we planning?" Lisa asked.

"Landscaping garden," he replied. The face she

made said he was in over his head, and her grin indicated she wanted to laugh at him, but held back because Emma was there. Oddly enough, her reaction made him want to laugh at himself. "And as you've probably surmised, I don't have a clue."

"And that shouldn't matter," Lisa told him smoothly, and gained another point when she tipped her gaze down to Emma's. "Because it's *her* project, right? That's why the 4-H leader sent you to see me."

It was.

Suddenly Alex felt a whole lot better. "Yes."

"Although a garden project this size is beyond the scope of a normal..." Lisa eyed Emma. "Ten-year-old?"

"Yes." Emma preened, just a little. "I'm kinda small for my age and people always guess wrong."

"Your eyes shine with ten-year-old wisdom," Lisa assured her. Once again Emma's smile blossomed into something Alex had missed for two long years.

"What we need to do is determine the amount of money you want to spend, the shapes of the gardens you're doing—"

"Redoing," Alex interrupted. "We bought a house on McCallister Street in February and while the house is in great shape, the previous owners had health problems and the gardens took the brunt of it."

"The Ramsey place."

They had started moving down a row of flowering perennials, following Lisa's lead, but her words stopped Alex's progress. "How did you know that?"

"Small town." She shrugged. "And I have friends a few doors down from you. Trent and Alyssa Michaels."

"Cory is my sister's friend." The new connection brightened Emma's face further. She looked up at Lisa. "Becky and my little brother, Josh, are at their house right now."

"That's perfect," Lisa declared. "Cory and Clay could use some playmates close by. That will keep them out of their big brother Jaden's hair. So." She faced Emma again. "Let's think about what your goals are, now that I know what house we're doing. Do you like bushes? Flowers? Easy care?"

"Yes."

Alex's bullet-quick response to easy care made her laugh.

And when she did a few heads turned their way, as if her joy inspired theirs. Another perk of small-town living, Alex decided.

"Easy care it is. And which sides are shady?"

Emma tapped her notebook. "The house faces north. There's a big maple tree out front and another one off to the side, so the north and east sides are shady a lot of the time."

"And the back? That's a southern exposure, right? Mostly sunny?"

Emma nodded. "It goes back to the creek that flows down to the Genesee River, so there's already a stone walk and a stone wall before you get to the creek."

"Which hopefully will help keep Josh out of the creek until he can swim," Alex added.

"And cost factors?"

Lisa angled her gaze up to Alex again, and her look of honest concern promised to work within the budget he set. He added that to a growing list of things to like about this woman and small towns in general. "I know things are expensive, but it's important to get it done right. Emma's pledged her whole summer to this project." He laid a hand on her head and she tipped a grateful smile up to him.

Her mother's smile. Beneath his eyes. So pretty, so sweet, too young to be touched by the realities of death at eight years old, but he'd had little choice in that matter. And she was a survivor. An optimist. The ensuing two years had made her more so.

Becky, his younger daughter, tended to take the world on her shoulders, more like him. And four-year-old Joshua just wanted to be loved. And fed. Often, if possible. Total boy.

"Well, you can see how crazy busy we are here today," Lisa explained.

Alex nodded. "Great for the bottom line, and that's important in business."

"It is," she agreed, but then placed a hand on Emma's notebook. "I'll give you ideas today, but if you can come back on a quiet weeknight, we can plan with fewer interruptions. I'm here every night this week. And I should swing by your place to get an idea of how you envision this going."

"Could we, Dad?"

"Well, I—"

"If time is crazy and today's better, we can get started now," Lisa assured him, and something about her willingness to help him, help *them,* made him more receptive to the idea of coming back. And maybe the pink barrage would be backstaged by some kind of yellow festival. Or purple. Even plain old green would be better than this immersion in bubble-gum-shaded reminders. "Monday afternoon?" He had Monday off so he could grab the girls from school and come straight to the nursery. "Around four?"

"That's perfect. And if it's all right with you, I'll come by your place tomorrow after church. For right now—" A voice over a loudspeaker summoned her to the front desk. Her expression said it had been a common occurrence that day. "And that's exactly why Monday would be better, because a project like this needs prep time. 4-H leaders look at the planning steps carefully. This is a big project for a ten-year-old." She winked and smiled down at Emma. "Even a really smart, cute one."

Emma grabbed Alex's hand. "Dad will help us." Her voice and gaze put complete trust in him. No way could he disappoint her on this.

"Considering the size of the Ramsey place, we'll need you to be fully on board," Lisa continued.

"While this is Emma's venture, she'll need some muscle to get the ground cleaned up. And then planted. And I'd love to be her 4-H adviser, but we have to have another adult on-site when we work on kids' projects in a private setting."

From a policeman's point of view, Alex understood the rule, but one look at Lisa's bright eyes and quick smile assured him his kids were safe around her. But something about the way that smile tugged his heart said *his* safety might be jeopardized. The awareness surprised him, but felt good. Real good.

Somehow feeling good felt wrong. Mixed emotions vied for internal control. He hadn't been attracted to another woman in a long time, but right here? Right now?

He was.

"That would be awesome." Emma's grateful gaze reflected his sentiment.

Lisa didn't talk down to Emma. Alex liked that. Emma's intelligence levels spiked the charts and he and Jenny had learned not to underestimate their firstborn. Odd but nice that this woman recognized Emma's gift from the beginning, but Alex found that some of his best detectives on the force came by the needed skills naturally. And that gave them a leg up. "Monday would be fine. And thank you, Lisa."

He stuck out his hand.

She took it. Smiled. Then did the same with Emma. "A pleasure doing business with you, Emma."

Emma's smile took Alex back to a time when smiles were a foregone conclusion and not nearly as appreciated as they should have been. "Thank you, Miss Lisa."

"Just Lisa's fine."

Emma's smile widened, the idea of calling an adult by her first name a thrill. Ah, to be young again.

When I was a child I spoke as a child...

His children had been pushed to grow up too early.

They turned to go, but Alex paused when Lisa called them back. "A quick reminder. Most plants grow quickly with TLC. Kind of like kids. So let's not overplan, okay? We'll measure carefully and see where that leads us."

Emma grinned and waved the notebook. "Dad and I will do that today."

"Excellent."

Lisa turned her gaze to his and waved, just a little wave, but her eyes...

Warm, brown, vibrant and full of life...

Said she was looking forward to working with them.

So was he.

"Who's the total stud-muffin?" Caroline Fitzgerald asked once Lisa cleared the main computer to recognize the tags on pink merchandise from matching vendors. On any of the vendors' products sold before the end of June, her dollar-per-item pledge toward breast cancer research would be matched with one of their own. Those donations could unlock an easier way to battle the disease. Something that didn't include radical surgery, poisonous drugs and radiation burns, treatments she'd endured firsthand.

This one's up to You, God. Put it on the heads, hands and hearts of those researchers to find a key. Amen.

"Hmm?"

"The guy." Her sister-in-law pointed across the sprawling sales area of their family business. "Tall, broad-shouldered, military hair and a soldier profile. With the cute kid."

"They're new in town." Lisa followed Caroline's hand motion with a quick gaze. "Alex and Emma Steele. Clearly you couldn't see his gray eyes from here, or you'd have mentioned them because they're heart-stoppers. Kind of calm and storm, mixed together. When he smiles, they brighten. Like when the sun peeks out on a cloudy day."

Caroline grinned at Lisa's elongated observation. "Really?" She drawled the word as if reading a lot into one simple statement about eye color, then paused, surprised. "Wait. That's Lieutenant Alexander Steele?"

Lisa's answering frown said she had no idea what Caroline was talking about.

"The State Troopers lost a bunch of people from

their investigations department. They transferred in several new guys from other sectors. If you listened to Adam more…"

Caroline's husband, Adam, was Lisa's younger brother, a great guy and a New York State Trooper, but between work, buying a new house and helping her father on the farm, Adam had been unavailable for much of the past three months. Work was the last thing he talked about when they were together. Lisa laughed. "And if there were more hours in a day…"

"I can't argue that," Caroline agreed. "Anyway, Alex Steele is the new lieutenant in charge of investigations. He's a widower," she added, but anything else she might have wanted to say was lost in saving her small child from possible annihilation. "Rosie-O Fitzgerald, do not even *think* of heading toward that parking lot."

"I've got her." Lisa snatched up the mop-headed tot and held tight. "I'm going back out on the lot to field questions, so I'll keep her with me."

"Thank you. I thought she'd be sleeping by now."

"She loves the limelight. Just like her daddy."

"Even though she looks like her Aunt Lisa."

Lisa couldn't deny it. Same dark eyes and dark curls. And she wasn't the only one who wondered if a similar fate awaited Rosie, if the genetic cocktail that had erupted as breast cancer in Lisa at age twenty-nine might linger already in Rosie's tiny, perfect body.

Cancer sucked.

Lisa tucked her niece onto her hip and headed back outside.

Crowds of people teemed around the displays. Her father was caught up in a composting demonstration beside the back shed, his go-green attitude prevalent throughout the garden lot.

Lisa headed toward the fountain exhibits. Landscape gardening was her forte, a blessing in more ways than one. Between losing her breasts, her lymph nodes, her hair and a husband who decided damaged goods weren't his cup of tea, she'd poured herself into fun landscape design.

Flowers gave her joy.

Gardens gave her repose.

Fountains offered hope of life-giving water, the image of Christ in the river, being baptized by a mere man, his cousin. Some of her favorite choir songs embraced water. Sacrifice. Rising to the challenges life set before you. She used to excel at the "faith-in-all-things" mentality. Lately?

Not so much.

Right now a neighborly challenge aimed her way. Chin down, eyes sharp, Eddie Jo Shupert wore determination like a mantle of clothing. The aged woman seemed certain that crises could be averted and illness made well by drinking her power shakes, three times a day.

Lisa reasoned that if the chalky-tasting shakes were God's answer to everything that ailed mankind, someone besides her neighbor might have figured it out by now. But since they were on a straight path for one another, Lisa had little choice but to paste a smile on her face and hope for a reprieve.

"Lisa! I've been hoping to talk to you! Have I got a great new line to show you, the kind of thing…" Eddie Jo lowered her voice as if sharing a compelling secret, for no ears but Lisa's. "That prevents *things* from coming back. Ever."

If only such a product existed. It didn't, but not for lack of scientific trying, and Lisa had no time to elevate this overture into a full-fledged conversation. Not on such a huge sales weekend with a wriggly child in her arms.

"Eddie Jo, you know I can't risk taking anything that might compromise the good effects of the medicines I'm taking. And I wish I could talk more now…" God would forgive her half truth, hopefully "…but we're swamped as you can see and I—"

"Lisa?"

A small voice called from across a clever display of pink-and-fuchsia perennials. She turned in time to see Alex Steele place a cautionary hand on Emma's shoulder, but Lisa didn't want him to shush the girl. Right now, whatever question Emma had was preferable to Eddie Jo's spiel. "Gotta go." Lisa gave Eddie Jo a quick smile and a wave. "Customers waiting."

She didn't turn to see if Eddie Jo looked exasperated. Eddie Jo was known to sputter, so it wouldn't be a news flash in any case. And Lisa held herself back from hugging Emma because that reaction would be over-the-top, but she realized Alex possessed perception beyond the norm when he quietly observed, "You owe me." His gaze flicked toward Eddie Jo before coming back to rest on Lisa. "I met Ms. Shupert in church last Sunday and was treated to an informative discussion on how using her products would not only improve my children's grades and hair texture, but establish good colon health for me."

"Good colon health being of great importance at church." Lisa met his naughty and knowing smile with one of her own.

"Right up there with teeth whitening and forgiveness," he agreed, his voice easy. The way he handled their banter, with quiet humor and intelligence, made Lisa realize Alex Steele was a breed apart.

She liked the tenor of his voice. The solid but gentle feel, very Roosevelt, the whole iron-fist-in-a-velvet-glove thing. He sounded strong but looked approachable, and that made for a wonderful combination. "You guys needed me?"

"It's about these." Emma pointed to the perennial area. "If this kind of flower comes back every year, why don't people just grow them? Why waste money on those?" She pointed to the greenhouses and tables loaded with bright-toned annuals.

"That's a great question," Lisa told her. She readjusted Rosie, plucked a coral-to-pink Echinacea blossom and handed it to Emma. "This is a cone-flower bloom. And it's gorgeous, it self-multiplies, and comes back every year, but it doesn't start to flower until mid-July."

"Then what do I do in June?" asked the girl reasonably.

"That's where the annuals come in," Lisa explained. She indicated the perennials with a quick thrust of her chin. "I've forced these indoors so people can get a visual of what their gardens will look like later in the summer, but you have to pick carefully to have a colorful garden from April through October. So most folks use annuals to add color because our gardening season is short."

"I didn't know how much flowers cost," Emma admitted. Her voice went softer. "Dad, if this project is too much for you, we can just do part of it. I don't want you to run out of money."

Lisa's heart melted. What a gracious child, to be concerned over her father's ability to pay. It almost made her want to cut him a deal, but if Caroline was correct and Alex was the new lieutenant in charge of investigations for Troop A, then he was doing well enough to make her income look paltry by comparison.

Therefore, Alex Steele would get no deals at Gardens & Greens, regardless of how compelling his gray eyes were. Or how adorable his kid was. To his credit, he shrugged off the girl's worry. "We're fine, Em, but I appreciate your concern for my bottom line. Is this your daughter?" he asked then, changing his attention to include Rosie. "She looks like you."

"My niece," Lisa replied. She nuzzled Rosie's dimpled neck and laughed when the little girl screeched. "I'm not married."

"Ah."

Why did I say that, why did I say that, why did I...

She hadn't meant her reply the way it sounded, like gifted information. As if she expected him to care whether she was married or not. That ship had sailed because she understood what few women knew: a spouse might claim to be in it for the long haul, but cancer had a way of changing things. In her case it took less than six months for Evan to dump her once she had to fight for her life at the expense of her breasts and hair.

"Well, she's beautiful." The look Alex shifted from Rosie to Lisa suggested he wasn't referring just to the child.

A flush started somewhere within Lisa, a hint of pleasure mixed with a dose of embarrassment because she hadn't been fishing for compliments. Conversely, she didn't exactly mind being on the receiving end of a delightful flirtation. A flirtation that made her want to smile more than she had in several years.

"Well, guys, if you don't have any more questions?" Lisa arched a brow to Emma.

Emma patted her notebook. "We're good. Thank you, Lisa."

"You're most welcome. I'll see you soon."

"Yes."

Lisa moved down the new brick walkway, a recent project designed to showcase the various applications of brick, stone and grass for garden paths. She felt his eyes watching her, wondering…considering…

But she refused to turn and see if her suspicions were correct, because as good as it felt to smile and trade quips with a strong-talking, gently spoken man like Alex Steele, she had no idea how to go about explaining what she'd been through. That she wasn't exactly the average woman next door anymore. If she was, she'd still be married and maybe have a few rug rats of her own running around the garden.

But she didn't and wouldn't most likely, even though the fertility clinic had harvested and frozen a clutch of her eggs before chemotherapy could destroy the tender information stored within them.

She was closing in on her five-year mark, a big deal in cancer circles. Five years cancer-free meant you might have really, truly won the war, battle by battle.

Each and every day she prayed that was true, right after telling God "Thy will be done" in the Lord's Prayer.

Where lay the truth? Was she all right with God's

will if it meant succumbing to cancer? Or was her earnest prayer for continued good health the more realistic side of her?

She didn't know. But she cared. Oh, yes. She cared a great deal.

Chapter Two

"Hey, Dad." Lisa hailed her father as one of the college guys maneuvered a watering hose up and down the aisles, giving the plants a much-needed drink while the sun banked west. "Amazing sales today."

"You're right." Her father slung an arm around her shoulders and gave her a half hug. "Mostly due to your efforts."

"Oh, please."

He squeezed again, lighter this time. "You've picked up a lot of slack around here this year, between losing your mom and my absent-mindedness."

"It's okay to grieve, Dad."

"I know that." He paused and let his gaze wander the pretty sight of the well-kept nursery. "This was her doing, you know."

Lisa had heard this all before, but if Dad wanted to tell the story again, she'd let him.

"I thought we'd do well with beef cattle. And we did, to a point. But then your mother branched out from gardening to plant production. Those first greenhouses…" He smiled, remembering. "You were just a baby and Adam wasn't born yet, but your mother and I fashioned them by wrapping metal poles around the silo with the tractor to get a perfect curvature. Then Uncle Dave welded them to the base frame. We added plastic sheeting covers and an old wood stove to maintain temperatures overnight, and a new business was born."

"It may have been Mom's idea, but your hand helps stir every pot on the place, Dad."

"Because I'm no fool," he declared, laughing. "And when you took after your mother, with that knack for growing things and promotional planning, I realized I'd be smart to be the brawn of the operation and let you two be the brains."

"I like the sound of that." She pointed to the back area, where piles of mulch outlined a large, curved loading area. "Which mulches do I need to replenish?"

"Black, red and natural."

She nodded and moved inside. "I'll email the order over so we have delivery by Monday. And we're okay on bagged varieties?"

"For now I'd hold off on the pre-bags."

"Gotcha. Hey, I'm going to the nine o'clock service in the morning."

He turned, puzzled, because the choir sang

at the ten-thirty service and Lisa sang with the choir. "Because?"

"I'm stopping by the old Ramsey place for a consult after church and I want to get back here early. If today was any indication, tomorrow will be cranking busy and I want to have time to meet people. Talk with them."

"Just like your mother."

He smiled when he said it, but Lisa understood the ache inside. The upcoming holiday would be their first Mother's Day without Maggie Fitzgerald. Lisa didn't want to think about it, and if keeping busy at the garden center kept the loss of her energetic mother off her mind, all the better, but it was hard when every flower she touched, every order she placed, every display she arranged reminded her of where her talent came from.

Her mother. Gone in her mid-fifties from debilitating heart disease caused by a blood infection. Who would have thought such a thing possible?

Not Lisa. Not after her mother had championed Lisa through two rounds of chemo, multiple surgeries and weeks of exhausting radiation. Maggie had been a go-getter who raised two kids and looked forward to teaching her grandchildren the ins and outs of the gardening business she loved. She'd lived just long enough to see Rosie take her first steps, a new generation of Fitzgeralds on the run.

And then she passed away, just after Christmas.

Lisa shoved the encroaching melancholy aside

and forced herself to remember the good times. Her mother was a staunch Christian, and a determined adversary of people who let obstacles mar their paths. Maggie's motto? *Go for it. Get it done.*

Lisa felt the same way, but that didn't ease the sense of loss. Still, keeping Gardens & Greens booming was the best way to salute her mother's memory and keep her father's grief sidelined.

Sunday morning chaos. How could someone who commanded a troop of officers manage to mess things up repeatedly on Sunday mornings?

And just when Alex thought they might get out the door for the early service at Good Shepherd, the doorbell rang. He looked out the window. His hopes for a quick getaway plummeted.

Jenny's mother. Here. In Allegany County. And of course the house looked like an F-2 tornado had just raced through, leaving a path of total devastation in its wake. And here was Nancy Armstrong, her new luxury vehicle parked behind his SUV, looking like she might be ready to move in.

Murphy's Law resounded in his brain: if something can go wrong, it will, and at the worst possible time.

He opened the door, wishing Josh and Becky hadn't picked that moment to mushroom their verbal argument into full-scale hand-to-hand mortal combat. "Hey. Stop it, you guys! Becky, let go of him."

"He took my game!"

"I wanna play Super Power Rangers!"

"Find yours!"

"You lost mine!"

"Did not!"

"Did—"

"Josh. Stop. Now." Alex plucked the scrappy boy up from the carpet and kept him out of Becky's reach, but it wasn't as easy as it used to be. Becky had grown, which meant a shopping trip and the ensuing arguments over clothing. Emma couldn't care less about what she wore, and if someone saved her the trouble of shopping so she could get lost in a book, all the better.

Becky?

Her word was law in the kids' department.

"Give it to me."

Alex plucked the electronic game system from Josh and held it up. "That's not how you ask for things, Becky."

"I shouldn't have to ask for it," Becky screeched. "It's mine! He took it!"

"I need it!" wailed Josh.

"Well, you can't have it. It's mine." Becky stomped her foot, arms crossed tightly over her chest. "And no one…" she angled a scathing look up, a glare that included her father and brother "…has my permission to use it."

Nancy's quick intake of breath screamed disappointment in him and her grandchildren's behavior.

Becky's decision to make a hard-line stance right

now was a big mistake. Huge. First to mouth off to her father, but second to do it in front of her disapproving grandmother. Nancy had suggested in the past that he would most likely muck up raising her daughter's children. The current scene gave him little room for argument.

She'd also opposed his decision to move the family to the more rustic, rural Troop A area. She'd accused him of running away. What she didn't get was how soul-tired weary a guy could get fighting crime in the city. Surrounded by need and want, desperation and dejection. Losing Jenny left enough sadness in his life.

He'd opted for this new setting purposely, a fresh start. Trees and hills. Peace and quiet.

Well, okay, that last was purely subjective, considering the battle of wills raging between his kids now.

He trained his gaze firmly on Becky, hoping she wouldn't pick this moment to dig her heels in. "Go to your room."

"No." She folded her hands tighter, thrust her chin farther into the air and tapped a foot. At that point she might have wanted to thank her grandmother for showing up unexpectedly because the kid had no idea how close to death she might be.

Alex set Josh down. Josh immediately tried to grab the gaming device, missed and managed to rake his nails across his father's chin instead.

"Oh, he's bleeding!" Nancy exclaimed. Her hand

flew to her mouth as though taken aback by the level of violence. "Alex, what have you done?"

"He's not bleeding," Alex replied, disgusted with himself for letting things get out of hand. "I am. Becky. Room. Now."

She glared at him, her expression mulish, her profile taut, as if she had a choice.

She didn't.

"Becky, maybe if you apologize to your father..." Nancy's unwelcome entreaty interrupted the emotional scene.

"Go to your room. If I have to carry you, you lose privileges for the week."

"The week!" *Stomp! Stomp!* "Because he's a brat? Because he takes things that don't belong to him? I get punished because my brother's a brat?"

"And we're done." Alex swooped down, picked her up, carried her upstairs to her room and left her alone to pitch a fit, which meant they'd be lucky to make the mid-morning service in ninety minutes. "I'll talk to you later."

Something sailed off the door. Alex reminded himself to be grateful for antique solid oak doors and hoped it was a softcover book. Hardcovers left bigger marks.

Engaging.

The Federal-style brick home epitomized grace, thought Lisa as she stepped out of her Gardens & Greens SUV. White-rimmed windows stood out against aged red brick. Evergreen shutters flanked sparkling glass, and each shutter featured Americana-styled inset stars separating the panels. A slate gray roof complemented the tones beneath, and shade trees, newly leafed, would offer welcome respite from summer heat.

Delightful.

Right until the front door burst open and a shrieking wildcat of a girl raced out, yelling naughty things over her shoulder. Delightful downgraded to wretched normalcy in the blink of an eye.

"Rebecca Eileen! Get back in here this instant, or I'll—"

Alex caught sight of Lisa. Surprise and chagrin mixed on his features. His shoulders sagged. He stopped, ran a hand across his chin and frowned, but was the frown from his forgetfulness or the current melodrama?

Lisa wasn't sure, but the look on his face said the morning couldn't possibly get worse.

Except it had with her arrival.

Which only made the situation funnier in Lisa's book. "Good morning, Alex. That, I take it—" she hooked a thumb to the right where a stubborn little girl, pigtails bouncing, strode down the street "—is Becky."

"That's her, all right."

Memories split Lisa's sympathies. She'd been the bullheaded one in the family, the scrapper, the fighter. Luckily she'd grown out of it, but maybe that doggedness helped her in her fight against cancer. Who could say?

Alex's expression said he hated being caught with out-of-control kids. Embarrassment and irritation painted stress lines on features that had looked pretty serene yesterday. Lisa moved closer and made a face of sympathy. "I'll come back another time. After you've had time to dispose of the body properly."

"What!"

Another voice entered the melee, a female voice, shocked and chagrined.

Surprised, Lisa stopped.

Alex turned.

A little boy voice whined, "Do I have to stay in these stupid clothes another whole hour?" Only he stretched the word *hour* into four elongated syllables.

"Nancy, this is Lisa Fitzgerald from the nursery Emma was telling you about." Alex offered the introduction through the screen door, so Lisa had no idea who Nancy was, but figured she must belong to the yacht-length elegant car in the driveway.

"Lisa!" Emma came around the side of the house, ran to Lisa's side and hugged her around the waist. "I'm so glad you came. Becky's acting like a—"

"Emma."

"Well, she is, Dad. And Grandma's here and we've missed church unless Dad makes us go to the other church where the screechy old lady sings songs I don't know so we've just about ruined Sunday."

Lisa looked at her watch. "You've got ten minutes to make it to Good Shepherd. Go."

"Go?" Alex looked at her, confused. A questioning look took in the wayward child two houses down.

"Yes, go. If Becky wants to come, I'll drive her over. If not, she can stew and be left behind. I guarantee she won't like that scenario."

"You're right," Alex admitted.

The smile she flashed him said she already knew that. "I'll hang out here and get measurements. You may or may not see her in church, but my guess is a big, fat no."

"I concur. Come on, Josh." He turned, opened the screen door and picked up one of the cutest little boys ever to walk the face of the planet. "Lisa, Josh. Josh, Lisa."

"Hey, Josh." She smiled at him, gave Emma's shoulder a quick squeeze, then paused when an older woman charged through the door looking ready to do battle with anyone in her way. Lisa wisely shifted left.

"You're going to leave Becky here? To miss church? That's not right, Alex, and you know it."

"Better than having a meltdown *in* church," he replied as he fastened Josh into the car seat. "And no reason to mess up everyone's Sunday. You sure you don't mind staying, Lisa?"

"I was going to be here anyway. It's fine."

Emma climbed into the back seat. "See you later, Lisa! Sorry about all the drama."

Lisa laughed. "Oh, honey, I was eight once. I invented drama. You go. Be good. Pray. Sing. Cut your father some slack."

"Nancy, are you coming with us or heading back to your motel?" Alex directed a no-other-options look to the older woman.

She pressed her lips together, clearly displeased by her limited choices, then shrugged, moved to her car, climbed in and slammed the door shut.

Ouch.

She pulled out, turned left and headed for Route 19.

Alex backed out, and turned right toward Jamison.

Becky stared, mouth open, her gaze taking in the family car heading into the commercial center of the village, the stranger in her yard and her grandmother's car growing fainter by the minute.

Lisa scored a point for the element of surprise, opened her no-line steno pad and started sketching the house layout. It took only a few moments before a small, impudent voice demanded, "Who are you?"

Lisa ignored her.

"I said, who are you?"

Lisa sketched swiftly, letting her gaze wander the home's exterior. "Great brickwork," she murmured, hoping her voice would ease the child's ire. "And those shutters… Marvelous."

"You like our house?"

Becky's voice softened. Curiosity replaced anger in her gaze, her stature. "It's lovely," Lisa replied. "I remember noticing this house when I was about your age. They had the most beautiful gardens ever. Mrs. Ramsey knew everything there was to know about flowers and shrubs and trees. She even had a toad garden."

Becky frowned, but drew closer. "A what?"

"A toad garden," Lisa replied, eyes down, continuing her outline.

"What's that?"

Lisa glanced at her watch. "Well, I'd be glad to tell you but aren't you supposed to be at church with your family?"

Becky flushed, then sighed. "Yes."

"I believe a deal can be struck, Becky Steele." Lisa stuck out her hand. "I'm Lisa Fitzgerald from Gardens & Greens. Your dad and Emma came to see us about fixing these gardens."

Becky nodded, excited. "We're coming to see you tomorrow!"

Lisa sent her a doubtful look. "Do you think your father will bring you after this morning?"

The girl scowled, remorseful. "Probably not."

"But," Lisa went on, as if she had nothing better to do than drive disobedient little girls around, "if you go to church now and behave yourself…"

Becky gulped, shrugged and nodded.

"Maybe your dad will let you live."

A smile blossomed on the little girl's face. A small smile, one that said she might have discovered a kindred spirit in Lisa and liked the revelation.

"Shall I drive you over? You won't be more than a minute or two late and if you promise to slip in quietly…"

"I will!"

"Good." Lisa closed the steno pad with a satisfied nod. "I'll explain about the toad garden when you get back."

"Oh, thank you!" Becky turned, ready to go, then stopped. "Wait. Do I look okay?"

"Here." Lisa straightened the girl's red bow under a slightly mangled collar. "Much better." Becky's patent leather shoes bore smudges from toe-dragging along the sidewalk, but right now, having the kid turn her behavior around was clutch. Lisa climbed in, thrust the car into gear and drove through Jamison. She pulled up outside Good Shepherd and watched as Becky bounded up the steps. At the top, the girl turned and called out, "See you after church!" in a voice loud enough to interrupt the five concurrent services neighboring the Park Round.

Lisa put a finger to her lips.

Becky clapped a guilty but cute hand to an "oops!" mouth, then tiptoed through the door. All Lisa could do was pray she'd done the right thing.

Guilt swamped her as she turned down McCallister Street.

She'd flirted with Alex. Teased him. Acted as if everything was normal in her world.

It wasn't, and between fighting cancer, being dumped then divorced, her brother's wedding and her mother's illness, she'd spent the last few years out of the dating loop, intentionally.

Alex Steele tempted her back into the mix, but how did a woman casually divulge that she no longer had natural breasts?

Awkward.

And the possible subsequent rejection?

That didn't make the short list, ever again. Evan's leaving had wounded more than her heart. It grieved her womanly soul, because part of her couldn't blame him. He hadn't signed on for damaged goods, a woman scarred and rebuilt. He'd vocalized his fears, that he couldn't live with a ticking time bomb.

Lisa shared those fears with one major difference: she had no choice but to live with the threat of recurrence. She'd taken upper level statistics, she understood the theory of likelihood, but she'd lost that game once already.

No history of breast cancer on either side of the family: CHECK.

No detectable genetic markers making her a likely candidate: CHECK.

No behavioral choices that made her more susceptible to breast cancer: CHECK.

She got it anyway. Lisa swallowed a sigh.

She was doing fine on her own. Working, creatively running a great business and filling some of the void her mother's death had left. Maggie Fitzgerald had been an avid volunteer, running school and 4-H programs. Lisa and Adam had the childhood blue ribbons to prove it.

But beyond that?

Lisa was better off keeping things with Alex Steele "business casual." Safer for everyone, all around.

Chapter Three

"Hard at work, I see." Alex softened the wry observation with a smile when he found Lisa lounging on his backyard swing after church. "Examining critical vantage points, I'm sure."

He moved toward her, bearing gifts in the form of twenty-ounce to-go cups from the village café.

Lisa waved her sketch pad in protest. "Good landscape development needs to be considered from all angles and heights, including sitting. Is that coffee? Please say yes."

He nodded. "I wasn't sure what you'd like…"

"Cream, sugar, shot of caramel or chocolate."

"The fact that you like frou-frou coffee is disadvantageous but I guessed correctly." He settled into the swing alongside her as he handed her the cup. "And I bought a third one, plain, just in case. These days, guys need to cover all the bases."

She made a face at him. "My coffee is not girly.

It's just delicious. And on a bad day I take an extra shot of espresso. Keeps me out of jail."

"You understand I'm an experienced investigator, don't you?" He made a warning face over the rim of his cup. "Anything you say may be used against you."

She laughed. "Charges vary depending on the occasion. Where's Emma?"

Alex waved his free hand toward the house. "I sent them to get changed. Which means their church clothes will add to yesterday's clutter."

"Because you were shopping for garden advice."

He accepted that, bemused. "I won't pretend I'm good at keeping up with things when I'm in and out. It's easy on my days off. When I'm working we fall drastically behind."

"Pay 'em."

"What?" He turned more fully her way, confused.

Lisa lifted her gaze to the house. "Give them a generous allowance to take care of things. Josh is little, but Becky and Emma are old enough to understand responsibility, right?"

Usually he balked, affronted, when someone told him how to raise the kids, but something in how Lisa said it made him more open to the idea.

Or maybe *because* it was Lisa saying it… He'd examine that more fully later.

"An allowance. I tried that last year. Didn't work."

"For how long?"

He cringed, knowing he'd caved too soon. "A couple of weeks."

Her expression called him out. Her eyes crinkled. He took a deep swallow of coffee and sighed. "How come you know so much about kids if you don't have any, Lisa?"

"Times change. Kids don't. My mother was good at setting the bar high but reachable. My brother and I learned to work and earn at a young age."

"Adam's a good guy." That's as much as he'd say because he realized yesterday that her brother was also a trooper, same area, different barracks. He'd heard nothing but good concerning the younger Fitzgerald. Solid cops employed a firm separation of work vs. home rule, but he'd have been foolish not to notice Adam Fitzgerald's work ethic, his high "answered calls" rate. "Your mom paid you to work?"

"From early on. Of course that's normal on a farm, but it taught us to respect time and money. If the kids have a list of chores, they can check them off each day and collect their pay at the end of the week. If things aren't checked off, no money."

It made perfect sense. And he had solid follow-through at work. Why was his follow-through more difficult at home?

Because he hated being the bad guy all the time.

Still, Lisa made a good point. A list, a visual… Becky and Emma might respond well to that. He nodded and sipped his coffee, feeling more at peace

than he had two hours ago. A quiet church service…a few compliments on his children's behavior from some sweet old folks…and now, coffee
with Lisa.

He felt almost serene.

The back door opened and the kids streamed out,
shouting their joy. Serenity gave way to mayhem,
but in a fun way.

"Lisa, you're still here!"

"Hey, Lisa, I was good! Will you tell me about
the toad garden now?"

"Dad, can I have another donut?"

Josh's face wore the white sugar remnants of his
first donut from Seb Walker's pastry case, and possibly the second if the telltale streak of chocolate
meant anything. "I'm going to bet you had enough
for now, bud. Let's get you washed up, then you
can play."

"Lisa, were you able to sketch the garden?"
Emma's bright voice reminded Alex that Lisa had
come to work. Even so, having her waiting in the
backyard, looking spring-morning fresh when he
first rounded the corner of the old brick house,
made his heart surge with delight.

He tossed Josh over his shoulder, hauled him inside and scrubbed him clean. He put the donuts up
high because Josh wasn't above helping himself
to a second brunch, then went back outside with
the preschooler. This might be Emma's project, but

Lisa made it clear that the whole family needed to be on board.

Therefore, sitting in on her session with Emma should be considered a requirement. And that made his Sunday morning that much brighter.

Lisa needed to leave, ASAP. Before Alex came back with his adorable son, before Becky won her heart by trying so hard to be like her big sister, before Emma grasped her hand one more time.

She needed to leave while she could still control the temptation within, the urge to test the waters with Alex and his beautiful family.

Billboard-size warnings blazed in her head. She'd faced the dragon of cancer head on, out of necessity. She wasn't a warrior or a hero. She had done what was required to live, but in this weathered yard she was surrounded by the reality of early loss. Three motherless kids. A widowed father. An empty seat at the table. A yawning gap in the car.

Inviting male attention was too risky. She needed to embrace that reality. She gave Emma's shoulder a quick squeeze and moved toward the road.

"We're all set? Already?"

The surprise in Alex's tone stopped her. She turned and planted a smile on her face as he came through the back door. "You snooze, you lose."

He didn't feign the look of disappointment, but when she glanced at her watch, he nodded, understanding. "Duty calls."

"Yes."

"So. We're on for tomorrow?"

The way he said it made their 4-H session sound like a date. It wasn't. "Four o'clock." She turned and shook Becky's hand. "Thanks for turning things around, kiddo."

"You're welcome." Becky's smile and the grip of her fingers said she didn't want Lisa to go.

Lisa had no choice.

"See you tomorrow, Lisa!" Emma grasped her other hand, then hugged her around the waist, and Lisa couldn't resist hugging her back. Such a little thing. A hug.

But hugs came with great expectations sometimes, and Lisa wasn't free to explore those.

Really? That's what you're going with? Her conscience prodded. *Do you think you're the only woman who's gone through this?*

No, but she knew the statistics. Better than they were a generation ago, but not great. Not when she held women's hands in hospice on a regular basis the past few years.

On top of that, how did a woman bring cancer and loss of body parts into casual conversation with a man who appeared interested? Right now, she was an eighth-grader, tongue-tied and awkward.

"I'll walk you to your car." Alex turned, still carrying Josh. The four-year-old squirmed to get down, but Alex held tight. "You can't be in the backyard without me, bud. Not until you're bigger."

"Stay with him." Lisa stopped, faced Alex and put a hand on the little boy's shoulder. "Give him some play time. He's been so good this morning."

"Mostly." Alex head-bumped the impish boy. His grin made Lisa's heart soften with yearning. Resolved, she resisted the urge to linger.

She raised her notebook higher. "Emma and I can plug this into the computer tomorrow and see what the landscape program suggests. Then we'll refine it together."

"I can't wait."

The way he said it…

Smiling. Deliberate. With his gaze trained firmly on hers, a frank invitation to think about him for the next twenty-eight hours…

Made her realize he wasn't the kind of guy to be put off. And she liked that about him. But she wasn't the woman he thought she was, and there was no changing that fact. She smiled, turned and headed for her car, sure he was watching this time, because when she climbed into the driver's seat, he'd come around the corner of the house, just to see her leave. And his smile…

Bright. Wide. Engaging. His easy gleam drew her in. Now what on earth was she going to do about that?

Alex pulled into the garden store parking lot at 4:05 p.m. Monday afternoon. The traffic off I-86 had slogged with slow-moving tourists visiting the historic villages of Allegany County. Tourists who should be mandated by law to drive faster.

He swallowed a sigh.

Was he nervous?

Of course not.

Then why—

"Hey, guys."

Not nervous, he decided as he climbed out of the car and answered Lisa's smile with one of his own. Anxious. Anxious to see her once more. To smile at her.

The thought surprised him because he thought no one would ever appeal to him again. Not after losing Jenny.

But something in his stressed heart felt better whenever Lisa Fitzgerald came around with her saucy grin. He wouldn't have thought it possible, but now?

He grinned as Emma raced around the car in a desperate attempt to beat Cory and Becky to Lisa's side. "They insisted on coming," Emma explained, as if the younger girls were there against her better judgment.

"I do believe I invited them," Alex corrected her. "And if they're in the way, I'll take them on a garden tour so you and Lisa can get your work done. And be nice." He added the reminder with a lifted brow that said he expected more of her because of her age.

She made a face, impatient.

At *him,* a New York State police lieutenant. Did the child not realize he carried a gun twenty-four/seven?

He met Lisa's look over Emma's head and the sparkle in her eyes that laughed at him, the kids and the situation.

Said she was pretty confident he wouldn't go to extremes without just cause.

"You got the measurements you needed yesterday?" he asked as the girls went ahead, oohing and aahing over the sea of unrelenting pink. Only today he barely noticed the calamine-lotion wash of shades, because Lisa's nature compelled him to look at her. And that felt too nice to be denied.

"I did, yes." She bent and picked up a stray piece of paper from the brick walk, stuffed it in the pocket of some well-fit jeans, and waved the girls to the right. "Head to the bushes first, ladies. I need your opinion on something."

The girls led the way, Cory and Becky skip-running along, heads bent, giggling and laughing. Emma followed with just enough disdain in her bearing that it was obvious she'd outgrown such childish antics months if not years before.

"Emma was bummed that her time with you was cut short yesterday because of Becky's tantrum. She made her pay the price for half the day."

"Poor Becky."

The direct look he sent her scoffed at her sympathies. "Poor Becky, nothing. Shouldn't she have outgrown this by now?"

"Ah, she's eight." Lisa shrugged it off. "All kids are know-it-all brats at that age. It's in the rule book."

"Boys, too?" He looked her way, and she jumped at the chance to best him, and that only made him smile more.

"Boys are brats from day one. At least girls grow out of it." She turned as they stepped onto the paved lot. "Although Josh has got to be about the cutest kid I've ever seen. With that shirt and tie he had on yesterday? Priceless."

He decided not to tell her that taking Josh anywhere in a shirt and tie made them a total babe magnet. It wasn't like he intended to use the cute kid to gain female attention, but he would have to be blind not to realize the effect. With Josh in a shirt and tie, women constantly stopped to exclaim how adorable he was.

Josh, not him.

But some of their looks said he wasn't all that bad himself. Seeing Lisa's sassy grin, he realized she'd appreciate the boy's magnetism for the joke it was. Alex was pretty sure not all women would get that.

Jenny would have. She'd loved to laugh with him. She took his serious job and serious side and made their lives humor-filled and easy care. Right up until the day of her death she'd tried her best to fill him with warmth and laughter.

Much of the joy had died with her, but it didn't feel that way today. Today he felt…better. Much better.

"Dad, can we go see the fountains? Please?" Becky grabbed Alex's hand and tugged him left. "Do you mind, Lisa?"

"Not at all. Emma and I need to make some choices. Then I'll input them into the computer program and see what it recommends."

"The computer plans the garden?" Emma looked deliriously happy at the idea of a machine doing the work for her.

Lisa laughed. "It gives us a launching point. And the hard work is yet to come. Soil preparation, weed killing and planting, then mulching. Then watering and more weeding."

"Good thing we didn't plan a vacation this year," Alex told Emma.

She nodded, serious. "It really is, Dad. The book from the library said new plantings require constant attention."

Alex didn't mention that he had no energy to plan a vacation after accepting this job with a new troop. Moving three kids. Buying a new house. Sorting. Arranging. He'd even gotten a few rooms painted on his days off.

Lisa put an arm around Emma's shoulders and hugged her, laughing. "I love this kid. You go on and do whatever you'd like, because Emma and I can talk gardens all day and not miss you one little bit."

He couldn't resist the gold-plated opening. "Not in the least?" He held two fingers up with virtually no space between them. "The tiniest bit?"

Something changed in her eyes. A hint of warmth and understanding read his not-so-silent message that maybe he wanted to be missed. Just a little. And despite her shadowed reluctance, he thought she longed to play along. She sighed, glanced away, then drew her gaze back slowly. Very slowly, as if fighting reluctance and losing. "A smidge. Perhaps."

"I'll take a smidge. For now." He let his gaze linger a few beats longer than necessary, letting her read between the lines, then smiled, grabbed the girls' hands and moved toward the fountain display, whistling. He hadn't felt like whistling in a long time.

But he felt like it today.

"Okay, we've got the basics." Lisa hit the print button on her laptop. "Now let's see what the computer gives us."

The printer clicked, whirred and whizzed as it delivered multiple copies of the basic plan.

"Oh, Lisa, I love this." Emma took the front view into her hands and her wide smile said they'd hit pay dirt. "I've never seen a prettier garden. Can we really do this?"

"If your Dad approves," Lisa told her. She had

gone with a medium level budget by downsizing the bushes and adding more annuals. Landscaping four sides of a house could be cost-prohibitive, and she didn't want Alex to feel shackled to expensive ideas. With a young family, things had plenty of time to grow before he'd have to worry about graduation pics or prom nights in the garden, snapping pictures of Emma in a fancy ball gown.

"How're we doing, ladies?" Alex's voice pulled Lisa back into the present. She laughed and waved him in, then made a face at his empty hands. "Did you drown them in my fountains, Alex? Please say no."

"Naw. They were good today so it wasn't even a temptation, but thanks for the idea. I'll keep it for future reference. Your sister-in-law…"

He arched a brow as if questioning the relationship or searching for a name. Lisa went to name first. "Caroline. Yes?"

"Took them for juice and cookies. That was after Becky noted how Emma got to come the other day when you were handing out freebies all over the place."

"Caro's a softie." Lisa winked at Emma. "I'd have let them starve." She turned her attention to the gardening layouts and handed a copy of the front and east side to Alex. "What do you think? This is without pockets of color from annual flowers."

"And life as we know it would be remiss without pockets of color."

She ignored that he was teasing her for her choice of words, and smiled. "Yes, it would. I love color."

"Especially pink," Emma added.

Lisa turned, perplexed, saw Emma's gaze sweep the outdoor displays, and understood the girl's assumption. Without pausing to consider the possible fallout, she took advantage of a God-given opportunity. "Oh, you think that because of our breast cancer campaign. I'm actually a bold color person myself. Reds, golds, fall tones. But when you've walked the walk, it's important to join the mission to find a cure, right?"

Emma stared at her, confused. And maybe a little nervous?

Alex's face stilled. He glanced around the office and paled, as if hoping he'd misheard. His crestfallen expression said he hadn't.

Pictures of the Fitzgerald family throughout the last ten years lined the walls. Local commendations, benefits they'd hosted, people they'd helped, the growth of a family business chronicled a decade of success. But in the more recent area, photos of Lisa with the telltale chemo hats lined the wall with all the rest.

A part of her hated those pictures. Another part championed them as a battle won. And the extra curl in her current hair was an interesting change from the straight locks she'd had for twenty-eight years. Soft curls and waves? She didn't mind them at all, but she minded the look that dulled Alex's eyes. The pain she saw on Emma's face.

Emma recovered first. "You had breast cancer?"

Always direct, Lisa refused to sugarcoat things. "Yes. Five years ago."

"Oh, Lisa." Emma reached out and took her hand. "I'm so sorry."

Lisa wouldn't have expected grown-up empathy in ten-year-old eyes, but Emma was a one-of-a-kind kid. "Thank you, honey. As you can see, I'm doing quite well now."

"I'm glad."

Emma's expression said more. Alex looked battle-worn and possibly shell-shocked, but Lisa had faced that reaction before. She'd seen it on her husband's face every day for nearly six months, until he packed up, saying he couldn't stand the idea of waiting around for her to die.

Yup.

She recognized the body language. And it still stuck a knife-like pain into her heart, because if the conditions had been reversed, she'd have stayed and fought with Evan.

"So." She stood, handed Alex the four sheets of paper, handed a second set to Emma, and said, "Let me know if you approve this, Alex, and we'll get things going. We've got a few weeks to get rid of old plantings and perennial weeds so we start out with good weed control."

"Good weed control is important," Emma told

her father, repeating what Lisa had explained earlier. Emma didn't appear to notice her father's sudden silence. Lisa couldn't notice anything else. "That makes our job easier in the long run."

"Weed control. Dig up old stuff." Politely dismissive, he held the papers up, moved outside, called for Becky and Cory to head for the car, and started toward the SUV. "I've got to get these guys home for supper. Thank you, Lisa. I'm sure this is all fine. I'll get back to you on the details."

Cool. Crisp. Concise. A business deal.

She felt ridiculously hurt, a ludicrous response, because she'd just met this man a few days before. Something in his face, the humor and warmth she'd witnessed made old wonders and wishes spring back to life inside her. And even though she couldn't act on those feelings, she couldn't deny it felt nice to be admired.

But he'd drawn the curtain closed on humorous repartee the minute he saw the pictures of her during her year-long fight. She'd refused to hide during chemo and radiation, and she'd scheduled her bi-lateral mastectomy for early January so she'd have plenty of recovery time without messing up Christmas-tree and wreath sales. She'd used all of her strength to battle this disease, and maybe win the war. Only time would reveal that.

She waved to the girls and walked back to the fountain area, avoiding Caroline and her father. They'd read her like a book. She needed a few minutes to recover, because somewhere inside her she'd known this would happen. Men didn't want damaged goods. Alex was no exception. And while it shouldn't matter, it did. And that came as a wake-up call.

She didn't bargain on meeting Adam near the mulch station.

He and Rosie came around from the back barn. The toddler raced for Lisa, arms out, eyes wide, her broad smile easing the sting of Alex's rejection. This was the reason she worked to raise awareness. So Rosie's generation wouldn't have to go through the rigorous treatments she'd undergone.

"What's wrong?" Adam's face said she hadn't done a good job of hiding her emotions. Given five more minutes, he wouldn't have been able to tell, but right now she was an open wound, raw and bleeding.

"Nothing."

"It's not nothing when it makes you look like you want to cry," Adam scolded in a none-too-gentle brotherly voice. "Who hurt your feelings? And where are they? I'll punch them for you."

"You can't. You'll get fired and then who will buy Rosie pretty dresses and fancy shoes?"

"You. You spoil her all the time."

"Love doesn't spoil children," Lisa told him. She sighed, rubbed her cheek against the toddler's soft, dark curls and shrugged. "I forget how cancer scares people. And then I see the reality in their eyes when they find out, and—"

"Alex Steele?" Adam interrupted her with a nod toward the road leading to town.

She nodded.

He rubbed his jaw, made a face and said, "Listen, sis—"

"It's okay, Adam. I get it. It's not like I haven't dealt with those expressions before. I'm a big girl. I can handle this."

"You *don't* get it." Adam looked torn, then lifted his shoulders. "I don't talk about private stuff at work. None of us do. When we're on the job, we stay on the job. Full focus. Troopers that lose their focus can get killed."

She knew that. They'd buried a young trooper two years before, a victim of a hit-and-run driver on the Interstate while he wrote out a speeding ticket. Focus was clutch in police work.

"But I know this much—Alex's wife died of breast cancer."

Lisa's heart gripped tight.

Her pulse bumped down, then up.

Realization made her feel foolish. She hadn't seen revulsion in Alex's eyes, on his face. She'd seen naked fear, a replica of the emotion she knew so well. Too well.

"She fought just like you did," Adam continued. "I know this because one of the other guys that transferred in worked Monroe County with him.

But we don't talk about it. We just figured he could use some prayer. And moral support. It's hard coming in as a boss in a new setting. Not all the guys are happy when outsiders are brought in. But we needed a new lieutenant in B.C.I., and Alex wanted a fresh start for his family. Something without reminders."

He'd lost his wife, the mother of three sweet children.

He'd changed jobs.

Bought a new home.

While she was celebrating her possible full remission, he'd been dealing with the opposite image in the mirror, the aftermath of a killer's success. His wife's death. Why her? Why not Lisa? Why anyone?

"Oh, Adam…"

"Don't tell him I said anything," Adam instructed her. "I don't want Alex to think I talk about him behind his back. Especially to my pesky, know-it-all big sister."

"I won't." She set Rosie down, took the little one's hand and moved forward. "But I'm glad you told me. Now I can be more sensitive to it if he lets me work with Emma on this 4-H project."

"Lets you work on it?" Adam halted her progress with a hand to her arm. "You think he won't?"

"If he doesn't want reminders, walking into a place like this…" She waved a hand, pointing out the obvious. "Pink banners, pink flowers, pink hanging baskets and breast cancer information at every turn has to be like walking the plank. A slow and painful process."

"Hey." Adam turned her around and his no-nonsense cop face said she'd better listen up. "You do great work here. And it's not like you guys are on different teams. You've just taken on the fight visibly, using the business to help raise people's consciousness. There's nothing wrong with that, sis."

She knew that. And she wouldn't change a thing, but now she realized why Alex looked war-torn on Saturday. And why the house of kids seemed chaotic on Sunday. And why he'd recoiled today.

She understood they were on the same team, in a way. But she'd survived.

His wife hadn't.

And that made being on the same team unbelievably painful for him.

Alex glared at the clock, thumped his pillow twice because once wasn't enough, then hauled himself out of bed the next morning. He thought he'd put sleepless nights behind him in Rochester.

Obviously not.

Lisa.

Cancer.

Pink.

The words dogged his morning routine. When Becky wanted milk, he gave her juice. When Josh whined about his game system, Alex didn't even make the kid say please. And when Emma asked an innocent question about the start-up date for the garden plans, he'd snapped at her.

Right then he knew. He couldn't do cancer again. He couldn't do the watching and waiting. Not up close and personal. Never again.

He'd pray for Lisa's continued good health from a distance. Which meant finding someone else to do Emma's project, but even a small town must have more than one able-bodied gardener, right?

With that plan firmly in mind, he parked his car outside the Fillmore station house and strode in, determined. Jack Samson, a long-standing investigator, gave him a high-sign as he wrapped up a phone call. Alex approached him, a coffee cup in his left hand, his laptop bag in his right, and a self-made promise to push all thoughts of Lisa Fitzgerald aside, no matter how hard that might be. "What's up, Jack?"

"Overnight grand theft of pricey gardening equipment."

"Gardening equipment?"

"Well." Jack raised his notepad and shrugged as he headed for the door. "Garden, farm, whatever. In this case it's both because Gardens & Greens is a farm that's a garden store, right?"

Gardens & Greens.

Robbed.

Lisa.

Alex's heart did a double take. So did his brain.

The thought that someone with ill intent got close to her. Close to her family...

Lisa.

He'd promised himself he'd stay away.

That pledge dissolved into dust at his feet as he hurried after Jack.

Jack turned at the car, puzzled. "You're riding along?"

"Yes."

The clipped word said Jack should leave it alone. Jack did just that.

He nodded, climbed in and started the engine, but a tiny smile quirked the right side of his jaw, the only side Alex could see. "Okay, then."

He'd accompany Jack, make sure everything was all right. That Lisa was all right. That no one was hurt. And then he'd leave.

One look at her face as they strode into the garden center office a few minutes later said leaving wasn't an option. Knowing her past and seeing the pain of the present stamped across her pretty face, he longed to hug her.

He couldn't.

His entire being yearned to comfort her, to pledge her safety, and yes, maybe even kiss that worry-furrow between her eyes, smooth it away.

Right now she looked like she could use a hero, but the cool look she passed over him as she locked gazes with Jack said he'd missed his shot by a country mile the day before.

Alex understood her reaction. He'd brushed her off when he found out she'd been sick, a coward's choice. But the tables had shifted this morning, because someone had tried to hurt Lisa and her family.

Despite his promises to stay away, Alex had realized one thing: no one was allowed to hurt Lisa Fitzgerald. Ever.

Chapter Four

Sixteen hours ago, Lisa was pretty sure she wouldn't see Alex again unless they passed on the streets of Jamison.

And here he was, a purposeful stride marking the reason for his visit. He looked...vigorous. Masterful. And completely unavailable.

Lisa trained her gaze on the slightly smaller, older man to Alex's left. He stuck out a hand, first to her, then her father. "I'm Jack Samson. This is Lt. Steele." He jerked his chin in Alex's direction.

Ozzie nodded, polite, then shook Alex's hand.

Lisa kept her gaze averted. The last thing she wanted to see was Alex's pity. Or fear. Or repugnance. Therefore she wouldn't look.

"So, what's missing exactly?" Jack flipped open a small notebook and withdrew a pen.

"Our three-year-old Bobcat and a brand-new zero-turn mower."

Jack whistled and arched a brow. "Ouch."

"And then some," Ozzie agreed.

Alex said nothing, but Lisa felt his gaze. She ignored the heat from his soul-searching gray eyes and reached across her desk. "Here are pictures of both." She handed them over. The Bobcat was a simple advertising photo showing the T190 in all its pricey glory.

Alex eyed the small tractor and grimaced. "This baby is nearly thirty grand new, isn't it?"

"Yes." Lisa replied without looking at him, but inside she wondered what he was thinking. How did she appear now that he knew she'd had cancer? That she'd gone through the same round of treatments his wife had endured with one major difference. Lisa was here to talk about it.

"And the mower?"

"It retails around seventy-five hundred new and we've only had it six weeks."

"Show me where they were parked, Lisa."

Her heart stammered.

Her pulse climbed.

She had to turn then, because Alex spoke directly to her. The take-command note in his voice said he'd done it intentionally, but Lisa didn't take orders well. Or shift gears quickly. Until he'd walked through the office door moments ago, she'd shoved aside the needle-sharp brush-off he'd given her the previous day. At this moment, every fiber of her being wanted to shout at him, at cancer, at the unfairness of life in general. But she'd dismissed hissy fits as a pointless exercise years ago.

"I'll show you." She avoided eye contact by leading the way to the mulching/stone area. The narrow display paths didn't allow the whole group to walk together. Jack and her father eased back.

Alex fell into step with her.

Was that chance? Circumstance? Planned?

It didn't matter. She had health issues he'd faced and lost. End of story. Except his sidelong glances said the story might not be over.

But it was.

The fact that he smelled soap-and-water fresh made him seem approachable.

He wasn't.

She'd seen that yesterday and his reaction to her battle dredged up too many memories of Evan's recalcitrance. Lisa had no intention of stepping before the firing squad of rejection a second time. The first time had been circumstantial.

This would be deliberate. Therefore, stupid.

"They were parked back here yesterday." Ozzie's voice held regret. He ran a hand through his thinning hair. "Adam's told me time and again to be more careful and I shrugged it off." His pained look underscored his feelings. "I never thought someone would just pull in here and grab stuff while we slept right over there."

Alex eyed the distance from the house to the barn. "Aren't the newer Bobcats keyless, sir?"

Lisa cleared her throat.

Ozzie scowled. "Yes. I converted the starter because the keyless entry was a pain in the neck. But then if I kept the keys in my pocket, people had to come find me every time they needed to shift something."

"So you left them in the equipment." Alex's observation held no judgment, but he quirked a smile to the older man, just enough to say he understood. "Adam will have a field day with that, sir."

"Already did," Ozzie agreed, looking pained.

Alex could tell that Lisa's father was a great guy, not like that was a surprise. He'd known Adam for months. And now Lisa...

He longed to pretend she wasn't there, a few feet to his left.

He couldn't.

He wished he could turn back the clock sixteen hours and banter with her. Watch the way the sun danced off those dark curls, hear her heartfelt laughter with the girls.

That wouldn't happen, either. His fault. But right now he had a job to do and that included keeping her safe. The thought that someone targeted her spiked his protective side. He swept a quick glance over the house and business. "Whoever it was knew what they wanted. And when and how." He stared at the ground, then moved down the stone lot surrounding the barn. "It appears he came in along the grass to keep the noise minimal. And with the increase of traffic on the Interstate this time of year, we get used to engine noise and tune it out. It's especially easy when you have fans or air conditioners running."

"Frogs," Lisa interjected.

Jack nodded. "Peepers."

"Yes," Lisa agreed.

"In English, Jack." Alex had no clue what they were talking about, and he couldn't bark at Lisa so Jack made a handy target.

"Lisa's ponds. The trees surrounding the house and barns. The water spillways she's created and the state-designated wetlands are over there. You could drive heavy equipment up and down this field at night right now, and no one would likely hear it. The frogs and spring peepers are that loud."

Alex shifted his gaze to Lisa. A tiny smile softened her jaw…a sweet, touchable jaw that could go stubborn in a flash. "He's not serious. Is he?"

She answered, but didn't turn away from Jack. "He is. So hearing anything even with windows open is unlikely in May."

Concern climbed a notch higher. "You don't leave the windows open at night, do you? The correct response would be 'no.'"

"To cool things down as the days get hotter. Of course we do." She shrugged, ignoring his concerns as if he hadn't dealt with every level of crime imaginable for the last fifteen years. "And last night was the first bogeyman in thirty-plus years, so I think the odds are with us."

Except crime didn't sleep. Alex knew that. And he understood her small-town cavalier attitude, but after last night's theft, he figured a dose of reality might daunt her Sunshine Sue outlook.

It didn't and that spiked an internal lecture he had no right to give.

He turned his attention to Lisa's father. Ozzie still looked miserable and Alex understood the older man's angst. Missing equipment at the height of their selling season? A rough go. "Have you called your insurance company?"

Ozzie shifted his gaze to Lisa, then shrugged. "If we make a claim this big, our rates will skyrocket. We're hoping to find the equipment."

"But…" Alex would love to find their stolen equipment and return it quickly, but the likelihood of that was slim and they had work to do. Wouldn't calling in the claim make more sense? That's what insurance was for, right?

"We've got an old small tractor in the barn," Lisa explained in a cool, polite voice. "Not as useful as the 'cat,' but we figure it will buy us some time." She addressed the group in general, not him specifically. They'd been there twenty minutes, and not once had she met his gaze.

Guilt built within him. He'd brushed her off after she'd spent years fighting a killer disease.

What a jerk.

Could he help his reaction?

No. And yes. The initial reaction had been automatic. Gut-fear, paralyzing and quick.

But being an officer trained him to move beyond the norm and analyze information. What a shame he hadn't taken time to do that yesterday. He'd turned and walked away, almost herding the girls into the car in his hurry to put distance between him and the disease he hated.

And that made him feel like a total loser this morning. Currently, Lisa Fitzgerald needed his help and maybe his protection. Like it or not, she'd get both.

A black van carrying a pair of crime scene technicians pulled into the back lot. The tech crew climbed out, all business.

Jack, Alex and Lisa moved to one side while the techies scoured the area, snapping pictures, scraping for clues. A young woman turned their way. "We're going to follow the path of entrance to its source. Maybe we'll get lucky and hit a spot where his tires left a readable mark. There's a small oil slick here," she pointed out several drops of dark oil about twelve feet from where the equipment had been parked. "Could be from the thief's truck. And to carry this kind of equipment, he needed a decent-sized trailer. Those aren't easy to hide. Unless he's not from the area, in which case he could be long gone by now."

Lisa's rueful expression said she'd already thought of that. So had Alex. "Thanks, Deb."

She offered a quick nod before she moved away from them, on foot.

"They'll walk the path?"

"Yes." Alex followed the technicians with his gaze. "You can't get a good read while you're driving. No matter how upscale our technology is, sometimes good old-fashioned police work solves a crime." He turned her way more fully, wanting her to look at him. "How are you doing?"

She kept her attention on Deb and the young man as they traced the trail of bent grass toward the adjacent hay field. "All right, considering." She glanced at her watch, whistled lightly and moved to her father's side. Voice low, she indicated the garden shop area with a jut of her chin and moved that way, without a goodbye or even an acknowledgement of his existence on the planet.

Much like he'd done yesterday, so he shouldn't be surprised by how much it hurt.

She'd taken his hint to heart and kept herself distant, exactly what he'd intimated. At the moment, his decision seemed stupid, shallow and supremely one-sided.

Seeing her, knowing her family had been victimized, recognizing her stoicism while she looked everywhere but at him, Alex knew he needed to be part of this investigation, if for nothing else than his peace of mind.

And the chance to make Lisa smile again.

Chapter Five

"Eye-sweet Lieutenant sighting, three o'clock!"
Caroline pseudo-whispered the warning as Lisa
rounded the cash register area half an hour later.

Lisa refused to turn, but had no choice when Alex
cut around a vibrant petunia display and stopped
in front of her. With the register area at her back,
and Alex standing rock-solid in front, Lisa had to
look up.

Calm gray eyes considered her. Did she imagine a hint of warmth, a gleam of concern? Nothing
more than the chivalrous duty of dedicated law en-
forcement, she told herself. Right until he gripped
her upper arms in strong, gentle hands. His touch
thrust her dreams back to thoughts of sweet endearments and ever-afters. Hands that cradled, eyes that
understood too much. "I will do everything in my
power to get your equipment back."

Endearments?

Ever-afters?

Lisa chose not to sigh, but she mentally laughed at herself, pulled free, sent him a polite smile and a quick nod. "We'd be much obliged."

He scowled.

She walked away, fuming inside.

He could have sent anyone to pair with Jack Samson on this assignment. Troop A had several knowledgeable investigators. Why him? Why…?

She ran into a solid wall of gray cotton. That smell…summer linen, on the line, sunshine and dew… Clean. Manly. Rugged.

"Before you run away—" he drawled the words, giving her time to realize how childish her behavior must seem "—I thought we'd schedule time for Emma's project. My work commitments are tough right now and yours are crazy this time of year, but if we synchronize things…"

Lisa had firmly wrapped her brain and emotions around the fact that she wouldn't be seeing any more of Alex Steele and that he'd find someone else to partner Emma on her project, so his words blindsided her. "You still want me to work with Emma?"

"Yes." He didn't pretend this wasn't a complete turnabout, and that honesty pleased her. "You surprised me yesterday."

The news of her cancer. She nodded, jaw firm, her gaze lifted to his. On this topic, she would not back down, ever. She might fight the flames of fear that licked inside, but on the outside? She was

Lisa Fitzgerald, Cancer Survivor, Warrior Princess! "Your reaction surprised me, so we're even. But this way, we understand each other."

"Do we?" His gaze wandered her face, his expression thoughtful. "Are you that intuitive, Ms. Fitzgerald?"

"On certain topics, yes. I realize now that you lost your wife to breast cancer. I'm truly sorry." She heaved a breath and hoped her look of sympathy said more than lame words. "When I hear that this horrible disease robbed a family of a wife, a young mother, I sometimes feel guilty for living."

Alex read the remorse in her eyes, and mentally chastised himself. Out loud he said, "I don't think we get to choose, Lisa. I found that out the hard way, and that's tough on a guy who loves to be in charge."

She acknowledged his words with a frown. "I ask myself that every day. Do I want God's will or do I simply want to keep on living? If the two are at odds, which would I pick? And what if there is no 'God's will'?" This time she met his gaze and the look of question said she'd been seeking answers for years and found none, very much like him. "What if the whole thing is a ball of chance," she continued, "and some of us just get luckier than others?"

Luck? Faith? Alex couldn't deny the sensibility of her questions. "The science side of me wonders the same thing. But the faith side says I need to man up. Stay strong. Because life doesn't come with guarantees, right? And I'm the faith model for three kids. If I crash, we all go down together. And I can't let that happen."

As Jenny neared the end, he'd known it was selfish to beg for more time… But he did it anyway, afraid of life alone. He had no magic words of comfort to wipe away Lisa's angst, so he came back to the subject at hand. "So. Emma's project. What's step two? And when can we begin? I'm working this weekend, but I expect you need to be here on the weekends anyway, right?"

"Yes. But later Saturday would work for the initial stuff. We don't want to wait too long. The sooner we get things in the ground, the better acclimated they'll be before temps get crazy hot."

He withdrew his phone and flipped to his calendar. "Saturday, four o'clock. What exactly does this entail?"

"Weeding and soil preparation."

He typed a shortened version into the phone.

She hesitated, and he realized he'd done a real number on her with his reaction yesterday. Today, seeing her, knowing her family and business had been targeted for crime, he wanted to watch her relax over a garden. Grin at his kids. Make Becky's perpetual frown disappear.

He hiked a brow. "Dinner at six?"

She started to say something, then caught herself and shook her head. "Not a good idea."

Alex arched the brow higher but stayed low-key and stretched out his single-word question. "Because?"

"You have issues with my issues. Shoot, I have issues with my issues. And I've been burned over this whole cancer thing before, so, yes. I'm wary. End of story."

She almost growled the last comment, and that made him smile. "Good cops learn to deal with issues. And you need to eat."

"I'm thirty-three years old, I've been feeding myself for a while, but thanks anyway. However, I would love to do Emma's project. That's it."

Alex feigned acceptance. The best investigators knew to plant seeds of doubt, guilt or need...then walk away, hoping evidence would come to them.

Mending Lisa's hurt feelings wasn't all that different, but he wasn't about to tell her that. He'd most likely find himself dunked in one of her water gardens.

No, he'd mend fences the old-fashioned way, with time and patience. She'd faced a life-sucking behemoth and won the day. It wasn't her fault that Jenny had lost her earthly battle. And didn't Alex try to comfort himself with the promise of life everlasting? Of families rejoined at some day and time?

Scant comfort when the nights are long and cold and the kids are in a funk, man.

He pushed aside his pesky conscience, but knew the truth behind the warning. And he realized he couldn't toy with Lisa Fitzgerald's feelings. That would be cruel. But he didn't want regret, crime or anything else to bother her. Ever. He had no clue what that meant but he bent a touch lower, met her gaze and smiled right at her. "I'll see you Saturday. If I have updates on this—" he waved a hand toward the back barn "—I'll stop by."

"Or call." She met his smile with a measured look of disinterest, but her dark brown eyes said maybe she'd like him to drop by and refused to say it out loud. It fed the flicker of hope he shouldn't allow himself to feel. What-ifs flooded his brain, thoughts of three kids dealing with cancer all over again, but doing Emma's project with Lisa didn't equate to a marriage proposal.

"We'll take it step by step."

Her look said she read his meaning, but the set of her chin didn't bode well and that made him wonder who hurt her that badly. He wasn't sure he wanted to find out.

His cell phone buzzed as he made his way toward Jack at the parking lot's edge. The nursery was quiet. The lack of people made the expanse of pink more intense, but he didn't cringe like he had the week before. Seeing Lisa's drive and devotion bridged his aversion. Or maybe it was the common understanding: they both hated breast cancer. She'd simply chosen to man the fight, head on. He raised his cell phone, saw his mother-in-law's number, held up one finger for Jack's patience and took the call. "Nancy, good morning."

"Hello, Alex. You're working, right?"

He couldn't blame her for wondering. His schedule had been choppy of late. Covering hours, changing his schedule to attend school functions. He used to be a stickler for organization. Now he was lucky to plan a day and have it work out. "Yes."

"I've just moved into a short-term rental outside of Wellsville," she told him. "And I'm on my way to check out a more permanent place with a local Realtor for a few hours, but I'll be done by midafternoon. I'd like to come by and make supper tonight. If that's all right."

He did a mental scan of the day. Becky had a Nature Lovers meeting after school and Emma was starting a campaign to get elected for student council for the following year, so she'd be on the late bus, too. "Both girls will be late. You'll need a key."

"I can swing by the station."

"Excellent." It wasn't exactly the truth, but he knew he needed to upgrade his relationship with the kids' grandmother. His parents were retired and living in Arizona. That left Nancy as the sole geographical Grandma, and grandparents should be an important role in a kid's life. But he didn't want Nancy's disapproval or bitterness over Jenny's loss to make things worse. "I'll see you at the station. Do you need me to buy anything?"

"Got it covered, so no. And thank you, Alex."

She shouldn't have to thank him for allowing her to visit the children. He knew that. But she could make their relationship easier by being nicer.

Like she used to be, he realized. "No thanks needed. It will be great to have supper waiting. See you soon."

"Okay."

He disconnected, saw Jack's look of approval and met it with a fake glare. "What?"

"You acted like a decent guy."

"Samson, I am a decent guy."

Jack acknowledged that with a half shrug. "When that chip on your shoulder isn't weighing you down, yes. A little less of that would help ease things at the station."

What did Samson know about it? About him? And why were they having this conversation?

"I lost my first wife when I was twenty-eight," Jack continued.

Alex's hands went still on the wheel. "You lost a wife?"

"Carrie." Jack drew a long, slow breath and worked his wedding ring in a circle. "She was driving I-90 outside of Buffalo and a snowstorm hit. Rapid drop in temperatures, black ice, heavy snow, multi-car pile-up. She lived long enough for me and Sherrie Lynn to say goodbye."

"I didn't realize."

Jack accepted Alex's words. "I had a lot of growing up to do. Like you, I don't like change. Like you, I tend to box things up. Organize them. All of a sudden I was a single father, a little kid depending on me, and couldn't find time to breathe much less grieve. I was working as a sheriff's deputy in Monroe County then."

"Why'd you switch up?" Alex knew that Monroe County had a strong force with excellent benefits.

"I couldn't stand being around reminders."

Another similarity. Alex swallowed hard and nodded. "I hear ya."

"But I forgot that some people like reminders. They need them. And that I wasn't the only person who lost Carrie. Her parents were crushed. Her sister was brokenhearted. Her younger brother never forgave me for taking Sherrie Lynn away."

"It's only a couple-hour drive," Alex protested.

"If you're too young to drive, it's a lifetime," Jack replied. He tapped the window as they turned toward Fillmore. "Loss is a funny thing. Everybody takes it different."

Like Nancy, Alex realized. "You're telling me that moving everything down here wasn't the best idea."

"It is the best idea for you." Jack hiked that left shoulder again. "But now you've got to work double time to make sure the kids are okay. And that your mother-in-law doesn't lose an entire family on top of losing her daughter."

Guilt prickled Alex's neck.

He'd been adamant about moving last fall. When this job opened up, he figured it was meant to be. Divine inspiration or happy luck, either way, the chance to move away from chronic reminders of Jenny, of the life they'd shared, seemed fortuitous.

Now it seemed selfish.

Jack turned his way as he parked the car. "Don't get me wrong, boss. You're the head of the family. If you crash and burn, everyone does. So you've got to do what works for you. But I found out the hard way that I should have eased that transition for others. Carrie's brother hasn't spoken to me for fourteen years. And her parents treat me with kid gloves, as if afraid I might get up and leave again."

"You remarried."

"Ten years ago. And Laney and I have two kids together. She adopted Sherrie Lynn. And that made everyone mad all over again, but repairing a family takes hard work. And tough decisions."

Jack's words touched Alex. He saw the reflective reasoning in the sage advice. "I need to try harder."

"Yes." Jack grinned and clapped him on the shoulder. "Said with the utmost respect for my boss, of course."

"Duly noted." A car pulled around back. A thick-waisted, middle-aged detective climbed out. He saw them approaching the building and made it a point to greet Jack, not Alex.

Sal Iuppa had applied for Alex's position last winter. Command's decision to hire Alex hadn't sat well with him, and he didn't do a whole lot to hide his disdain. He knew the area, inside out and backwards. He thought his knowledge should have put him in the driver's seat. The command thought otherwise, but several of the guys agreed with Iuppa. In their opinion, a guy who'd done his years of service in urban Monroe County didn't have a clue how things should be done in the Southern Tier.

Nancy's car pulled into the parking lot behind them. Alex strode her way, removed a key from his chain and handed it to her through the open driver's-side window. "Thank you for doing this. And would you mind throwing a load of whites into the washing machine? Josh has Super Tot Soccer tonight and I forgot to wash his uniform."

"I'd be glad to." Her gaze brightened. Her eyes shone. And Alex felt like a heel for refusing all her offers to help. What kind of moron was he, thinking he had to do everything alone? "I'll see you later," she told him. "Do you want me to pick up Josh from school?"

"Yes." He said the word so fast that she laughed, and he couldn't remember the last time he heard Nancy laugh. "It takes me twenty minutes to get him out of the place. He drags me around, wanting me to talk to everyone. Meet the parents. I get home so late it throws off the entire evening when someone has sports. Or dancing lessons."

"I'll pick him up a little early, then," Nancy promised. "Can you call the school and let them know?"

"Will do."

"Okay. See you tonight."

She pulled out of the lot smiling, and Alex felt a twist in his chest as he watched her go. Like maybe his heart was unclenching a little control by letting Nancy help.

He turned and saw Iuppa's profile. Would the same maneuver work with the older investigator? Would added responsibility make him feel more valuable or have the opposite effect? He wasn't sure. He didn't want to complain to command. That wasn't his style. But he sensed Iuppa's simmering discontent would erupt at the worst possible time. He wanted to nip that.

Jenny had balanced his controlling side by thwarting it daily. Her maneuvers worked, even though he fought her haphazardness. She'd tempered him, which meant he'd been out of sync for over two years.

Funny how life had suddenly seemed more normal the day he met Lisa Fitzgerald at the garden store. As if his scales balanced again. Until he realized she'd fought cancer and won, for now. Uncertainty held him back, while her smile drew him forward. But today there had been no smiles. Nearly forty grand in valued equipment had disappeared. He needed to find that machinery and get it released into their keeping, ASAP, if only to see Lisa relax a little.

He'd hurt her.

Then she got robbed.

Now it was his job to fix both things, and in all honesty he didn't have a plan for either. Which meant he needed to get to work.

Chapter Six

An old man, assaulted, beaten and robbed of less than thirty dollars. Two high-dollar reports of vandalism in sleepy college-town Houghton. And someone in the tri-county area was running a meth lab with record distribution rates.

No way would he make it home in time to work with Emma and Lisa on the garden plan, Alex realized by noon on Saturday. Jack Samson's wife had been taken to the hospital mid-morning with chest pain. Another guy's wife was in labor in Jones Memorial. Alex was no stranger to double shifts, but not today.

Yes. Today.

He scowled, reached for the phone and hit Lisa's number. She answered on the first ring, which meant what? Something? Nothing?

"Alex. What's up?"

Her lack of inflection said he was just another business call. That disturbed him. "I'm short-handed at work and the world picked today to go on a crime spree. I'll never make it home by four for the gardening session. I'll be lucky to make it home by seven when George Novinski comes in to work, and that's only if I can bring paperwork with me."

"We'll reschedule." Background noise muffled her answer. Alex had no trouble picturing the thriving garden store on a height-of-the-season Saturday. "Call me tonight." *Click.*

She hung up on him.

She was busy, his conscience scolded.

So was he.

She said call her later...

But he liked to be in charge. To set the tone. To command the situation.

Too bad.

"Twila, it's Lisa."

"Hey, purty girl!" Twila Buford's voice squealed with delight. "Why are you calling me on a busy Saturday? I cannot believe you don't have customers clamorin' to buy your precious blossoms!"

Then and there Lisa decided she should record Twila-isms to play back in times of need because the old woman's twang and phrasing always made her feel stronger. "We need an emergency session of the Weed Stealers this afternoon, four o'clock, 118 McCallister." The Weed Stealers was a local group of good-hearted people who surreptitiously helped others with necessary yard work. They joined forces as needed, slipping in, doing the job and moving on, no thanks required.

"Where that fine-lookin' lieutenant lives with all them sweet babies!" Twila's voice crooned approval. "Mmm, mmm, mmm, I will get on the phone ASAP. Does Mr. Policeman know we're coming?"

"No." Lisa pressed her lips together, thinking, then went on, "We'll surprise him like we usually do. I was scheduled to work with Emma, the oldest daughter on a 4-H project, but her father is caught up at work."

"Oh, there's been goin's on!" Twila's voice rose. "I've had the scanner goin' all mornin', and I'm not surprised that the good lieutenant is in the thick of things. What are folks thinkin' these days?"

Twila was a no-nonsense person. If today's happenings roused her concerns, then poor Alex must really be up to his neck in work. "I don't know, Twila, but if you could gather a half-dozen people, we can make short work of this part of the job. I hate to disappoint Emma, and if Alex's schedule stays frantic for whatever reason, we could lose the best window of time to get things in the ground."

"I'm on it," Twila promised. "Four o'clock, the lieutenant's house. We'll be there."

Her promise eased Lisa's concern. Landscaping early wasn't a problem in the Southern Tier, but the closer they got to the unrelenting heat of summer meant struggling root growth. Constant watering. Extra work. A single dad did not need extra work. And Lisa wanted this garden to thrive for Emma's sake.

And hers.

She swallowed a sigh, shoved her competitive nature into a holding pattern and refused to dwell on why she wanted to look good to Alex Steele. She had nothing to prove to him and no reason to try.

Except that her heart had softened when he grasped her arms on Tuesday. And delight hiked her cardiac rhythms when she saw his name in her cell phone display earlier.

She'd tamped down both reactions and stayed calm and cool. And that's how things would remain because she'd been tossed aside once. On top of that, she'd been dealing with a dull ache, off and on, low in her abdomen. Annoying, mostly, but troubling, too. The chemo pills that helped block estrogen-receptive cancer elevated her risk of uterine cancer. At age twenty-nine, she'd been called on to make life-and-death decisions, one after another. She'd done it because it was necessary, but hated every minute of the process. And now...

You're borrowing trouble. You've done this before. Call the doctor, set up an appointment and be done with it.

A part of her wanted to do that. A bigger part held her back. Was she afraid?

Yes. Absolutely. Unequivocally. She was short months away from her five-year mark, the standard measure for success in cancer circles. The idea of wrestling another cancer?

Repugnant. Which didn't mean she wouldn't do it if necessary, but she hoped and prayed it wouldn't be.

I must be missing the spot where prayer came into this, her conscience scolded again. *Was I sleeping, perchance?*

Lisa ignored the internal reprimand because she heard it way too often. Sure, she sang in the choir, lifting her voice in sweet notes of praise. Externally she looked good. Faithful. Invested.

Internally?

She was a mob of questions with few answers.

She called Alex's Saturday sitter, discovered the kids were at the Michaels's house down the road, and called her second cousin Alyssa. "Hey, it's Lisa. Can I spring Emma from your care later today? We're doing a garden project together and I've arranged for the Weed Stealers to help us, but it's a no-go if Emma's not on hand."

"And surprise Alex?" Alyssa asked. "Absolutely. He could use a few nice surprises. What time are you guys meeting?"

"Four. Can you have her walk down when you see my car?"

"Will do. And I'll send the spare key in case anyone needs to get inside. And Lisa?"

"Yes?"

Her cousin's note of approval came through loud and clear. "Thanks for what you're doing."

Lisa hoped and prayed it was the right thing. Alex liked control. She recognized that. Admired it, even. But in the finite world of northern gardening, plants thrived more readily when done in a specific time frame. And that was her expertise. "Let's hope it's the right thing. Alex isn't accustomed to having people do things for him. Take charge."

Alyssa laughed. "Right on both counts, I'd say. But this will give him a hint of small-town living at its best."

"I hope so."

Lisa hung up the phone, spent the afternoon working the sales lot and arrived at Alex's home at three forty-five. She turned as an aging car drew up to the curb. An older woman climbed out, grabbed a pot and started up the drive.

"I brought supper." Weed Stealer Evelyn Calhoun made the announcement in a voice more cheerful than it used to be. "And a helper." Her quick smile indicated her granddaughter Sophie.

"Sophie!"

"Emma!"

Shouts of delight split the hot day as Emma raced down the street. Lisa shot Evelyn a smile of appreciation while Emma took Sophie on a weed tour. Evelyn replied by sweeping the unkempt garden plots a thoughtful look.

"Daunting?" She met Evelyn's gaze as two more cars pulled up to the curb.

"Dot Ramsey had a knack for all this." Evelyn took in the small beds marking the outside perimeters of the oversize lot and the ones framing the old brick colonial. "But when things get let go, it's a mess, ain't it? We should have taken this on last fall."

"Evvie, you old bird, you were a crank last fall," Twila griped good-naturedly as she approached them. "We wouldn't have gotten you on your hands and knees pullin' weeds here or anywhere else. And now just look at you." Twila's approving grin took the sting out of her teasing. "Totin' supper and ready to get dirty. Aren't you a wonder?"

Evelyn took the friendly jabs with a smile. "Amazing how nice you get when heaven draws close, isn't it?" She smiled over her shoulder to Lisa and put the Crock-Pot in the kitchen. "And it was Meredith that sent the food. She's at the spa all day and said Cam can throw burgers and hot dogs on the grill tonight instead."

"She sent their supper over? How nice of her." Her daughter-in-law's simple act of kindness would perk up Alex's elongated day.

"Sweet-and-sour chicken barbecue," declared Evelyn. "Four ingredients, best ever and guaranteed to please a man. Not that anyone here—" she slanted a nonchalant look in Lisa's direction "—is trying to impress a man. But Meredith saw how hard things were for Cam, raisin' them girls on his own."

Cam Calhoun had lost his wife early in their marriage. He'd been a single dad of two beautiful, athletic daughters for years, until Meredith came back to town to open a spa. Now they were happily married and the girls played great soccer and had really good haircuts.

"God's got his own brand of timing, don't he?"

Lisa choked back her true feelings, that God's timing wasn't all that high on her list. Not when she'd buried her mother five months back. Not when she worked to keep a smile on her face and shoulder extra work because her father's grieving took precedence over hers. As it should, she reminded herself.

"You got us organized yet?"

"I do." Lisa shook off the funk and refocused on the day. She paired up people and set them to work. As she did, another car pulled into the driveway.

"Grandma!" Emma raced across the lawn and gave Alex's mother-in-law a hearty welcome.

Emma's grandma looked around, puzzled, then walked toward Lisa, one arm snugged around Emma's narrow shoulders. "What's going on?" Her expression matched the concern in her voice. "Is something wrong?"

"No." Lisa indicated the yard with a thrust of her chin. "Emma's dad got tied up at work and we need to get the ground prepped for her gardening project. You have stumbled onto an emergency meeting of the Greater Allegany Weed Stealers Society."

Nancy laughed out loud. "What a clever idea! May I join you?"

"All are welcome," Lisa assured her. "Would you like to pair up with Emma and Sophie?"

"That would be perfect."

Joy softened the longing in the older woman's voice. Her little hesitation told Lisa she was uncertain of her role in the new family dynamic.

After fighting cancer and losing her mother, Lisa understood. Loss changed so many things. Her illness had thrust her no-nonsense side to even greater pragmatism. Losing her mother had pushed her to deeper sentimentality. Her regular chemo regimen messed up her hormones enough to inspire tears when there was no reason to cry. She defined "mixed emotions."

Nancy had lost more than a daughter. The link with her grandchildren had thinned with Jenny's death. Maybe with time and greater proximity, those ties could be strengthened again.

In less than two hours six adults and two little girls had the perimeter of the house ready for planting, while two other volunteers hand-weeded several of the smaller beds dotting the yard. "Take care on that one," Lisa reminded her uncle Gary Langley as he attacked a crescent-shaped, stone-lined plot. "Beneath the quack grass and dandelions lies a lovely herb garden."

"I'll save what I can," he promised. By six-thirty they had things in tip-top shape. Rakes, shovels and trowels were stowed for the next Weed Stealers gathering. The gathered adults had left. Not a trace remained of the impromptu meeting when Alex pulled into the yard at seven-twelve.

Lisa slung an arm around Emma's shoulders and watched Alex alight from the car. Would their efforts gain approval?

"Whoa."

Alex's eyes swept the house and the yard. Puzzlement gave way to happiness. He strode forward and locked gazes with Lisa. "How did you manage this?"

Off-limits, off-limits, off-limits...

Obeying the internal scolding, she gave Emma a half hug and kept things simple. "We rallied the troops. Nice, huh?"

"Not nice. Amazing." He bent and hugged Emma as Becky and Josh tumbled out of the car and marveled at the difference.

"We started a compost pile in the back," Emma explained. She grasped Alex's hand. "Come and see."

He dropped his work case onto the steps and trotted toward the creek side of the house, Emma's hand wrapped in his. The visual, father and daughter, running together... Lisa's heart softened at the sweetness of the moving portrait, oblique rays and cooling temps creating a creek-spawned mist wrapped around thick, mature trees.

"Lisa, I love this!" Becky exclaimed. She twirled around, arms out, her over-the-top reaction embracing life. Just as it should, Lisa thought.

"I'm glad, honey."

"Can I be here when we plant stuff?" Becky kept pace with Lisa as she packed her car with the last tools. "I want to learn, too."

"If it's all right with your father." Lisa lifted a questioning gaze to Alex as he and Emma approached. "When we start planting next week, can Becky help?"

"As long as it's okay with Emma." Alex shifted his gaze to his oldest. "What do you think?"

"Yes. But I'm still in charge, okay?"

"Sure!" Becky's face lit up. Eyes wide, she raced around the yard as if the clean flower beds opened a new perspective. Lisa understood her reaction. She'd loved helping her mother as a child, tackling jobs too big for her age. She saw that in Emma and Becky, but with differing applications. Emma loved the planning and development stages of the garden. Becky had the urge to get down and dirty, meeting the soil up close and personal.

A hand touched her face. Alex's hand. He smoothed his thumb over the edge of her nose, then her ear. Humor and something else softened his gaze. "Dirt."

She kept her smile nonchalant and stepped back. "Occupational hazard. I'll see you guys next week."

"Do you have to leave?"

A loaded question for sure. She didn't need to leave. The garden store was closed and her father was having supper with Adam, Caro and little Rosie. The night was hers. But should she spend the evening with this handsome, humorous widower and his three engaging children or home with a book?

The book won. Immersing herself in fiction made more sense than dangling untouchable possibilities in front of her face. She met his gaze slowly, resigned. "Yes."

"Sophie's grandma brought supper." Emma thrust the words into the void between the two adults. She grabbed Lisa's hand. "She said there's plenty for leftovers, so why don't you stay and eat with us, Lisa?"

"Yeah, Lisa." Alex squared his shoulders, leveled his gaze and held hers hostage. "The kids would love that. Me, too."

His eyes said he meant the words, but—

"Lisa, Dad's going to build me a tree house over there. Come and see!" Josh interrupted the weighted question by barreling into Lisa's side like a small freight train.

"Whoa, buddy." Alex squatted low. "We've got to be gentle with women. Remember?"

Josh tipped his gaze up to Lisa. "Sorry. Can you

come with me? See where my dad wants to build it? Because you don't want to plant flowers under a tree house. We might hurt them climbing up and down."

"He's got a point." Alex caught her hand. "Stay for supper. Check out the kid's tree-house plan. Relax with us a little. It's the least I can do when you've—" his look swept the transformed yard "—done all this. Please?"

Awareness swept her. Warmth stole upward from her fingers as his strong grasp and big hand engulfed hers. He was holding her hand. Asking her to stay. Josh grabbed the other hand, a mini tug-of-war between father and son with her in the middle.

And it felt good. And right, even though it couldn't ever be right.

"Ice cream." Chagrined, Alex dropped her hand, dashed across the yard, whipped open the car door, grabbed out a bag, frowned, then sighed in relief. "Not melted. Excellent. If it had melted, I'd blame you." He raised the bag toward Lisa as if displaying Exhibit One in a high-profile trial.

"Me? Why?"

"Because I tend to forget things when you're around, Lisa."

Oh, those words. That look. Soft. Engaging. But all man.

"Will you stay?" Becky added her plea to Josh's entreaty. "We didn't get to have any time with you, and Josh and I like being with you."

Her words softened an old ache surrounding Lisa's heart.

"And could you braid my hair later?" Becky implored. "Please? Dad's hands are too big."

Alex's hands weren't too big, thought Lisa. They were just right. Strong. Athletic. Broad. Gentle, but firm.

Alex hurried the ice cream inside, then reappeared in short order. "Something in there smells great."

"Barbecued chicken," Emma explained.

"Mrs. Calhoun brought rolls, too," Lisa added, although it felt silly to talk about rolls and chicken when a part of her wanted to talk about everything else. Or nothing at all. "And potato salad."

"So, you'll stay."

He didn't ask this time. Lisa liked that hint of commander about him. He'd had enough indecision and was ready to move on.

So was she. "Yes. Come on, Josh." She let the four-year-old lead her across the yard as fast as his legs would go. "Let's see this tree."

The smack of the screen door said Alex had gone back inside.

Barbecue. Ice cream. Hot sun, cool shade. Tipping shadows, slanting the yard with dancing light. Emma's voice, excited, leading Alex around the house. Becky's exclamations as they went. And Josh's little hand clutched in hers as he led her to the aged oak that skimmed the east-side property line. Right now this felt about as perfect as life could get.

She knew better. She and Alex had learned the hard way that expectations could crash and burn. But here, in this moment, the sounds, scents and scenes of a family summer unfolded around her. And it felt better than she'd ever thought possible a few weeks before.

"Delicious." Alex eyed the Crock-Pot, then his plate, and sighed. "We put a serious hurting on that meal."

"What does that mean?" Josh peered at his father and made a face. "Why would we hurt the food somebody brought?"

"It's an expression," Lisa told him. She reached over and swiped a smear of barbecue sauce from his face. "It means we liked it a lot."

"Like saying something's 'sick' when you mean amazing," Emma explained.

Josh rolled his eyes. "You could just say what you mean, couldn't you?"

The perfect teachable moment, Alex decided. He leaned over and met his son's gaze. "That would be too simple, my boy. And when you're dealing with women..." He lifted a slow, easy gaze that swept Lisa, Becky and Emma. "It doesn't hurt to have an interpreter around to figure them out."

"Hey."

"Hey!" Emma joined Lisa's softer protest and

smiled like she used to before Jenny's illness and death robbed part of her childhood. "Dad, did you know that Grandma came and helped today?"

"She did?" Surprised, Alex stood to gather plates. Lisa put a hand out to stop him. He turned, puzzled.

"Emma's clearing and rinsing. Becky's loading the dishwasher."

"Oh." Alex gave the list on the wall a quick glance. "I forgot."

"If you do our chores for us, we'll never raise enough money for a dog," Becky scolded.

Emma stopped, surprised, lips pursed. A light whistle sounded through her teeth.

Becky clapped a hand to her mouth. She flashed Emma a look of consternation. Emma returned it with one of overdone impatience.

They wanted a dog. And the reason they wanted a dog and were afraid to tell him was because he'd given away their oversize puppy when Jenny went into hospice. He hadn't been able to deal with three little kids, a dying wife, a job and an overzealous, playful eight-month-old pup with a penchant for destroying couch cushions, books, screen doors and sneakers.

From the looks on his daughters' faces, they still missed the puppy.

Guilt stabbed again. He should have hired help. He should have crated the dog more often. He should have—

Lisa's voice interrupted his internal scoldings.

"Why don't you and I take a walk outside while the girls finish up? Josh? Would you like to come, too?"

"Yes." Josh grabbed his baseball mitt and a ball. He tossed a larger mitt to Alex. "Can we play catch, Dad?"

"Sure." Alex swung the door wide. He let Lisa pass through, then Josh, but once they were outside, he caught up with them and reached for her hand. "Nice save."

She made a face toward the house. "Losing someone you love has so many ripple effects. And you don't know which ones will be most harmful until it's too late to change them."

"I shouldn't have given away their dog."

"Oh, Alex." She smiled up at him and in that smile he saw the compassion of a woman who didn't stand in judgment. A woman who understood like no one else could because she'd walked the walk. "I wish you could see how well you've done. You're a perfectionist."

Was he? Well, yes. Kind of. "In some ways."

Her deepened smile acknowledged the understatement. "When perfectionists get hit with things they can't control, they run around trying to control what they can. Eventually they realize they're not quite as all-powerful as they once believed."

"You discovered that while fighting cancer?"

She turned more fully to him as Josh moved several yards away, getting ready to throw the ball. "And while nursing my sick mother. And when my husband realized he couldn't handle a bionic wife who may or may not be a ticking time bomb."

"You were married?"

"Yes."

"He left because of your cancer?" Derision that anyone could do that ignited a deep-seated anger. The intensity of the sentiment surprised him.

Lisa's gaze stayed calm as she nodded, but he had no problem seeing the old pain in her eyes. He had to fight the urge to soothe that hurt away. Brighten her gaze.

"Dad! You ready?"

Josh's voice ended the conversation. Lisa stepped to one side and smiled as the little boy pegged a not-so-accurate throw to Alex. Alex scooped the ball off the ground and returned the throw gently.

Josh missed, but grabbed the ball up and threw it back.

Lisa relaxed into one of the twin Adirondack-style chairs flanking the fire pit. She smiled as they tossed the ball, and when Josh finally caught one in his mitt, she jumped out of the chair, fist-pumped the air and squealed as if the kid just hit one out of the park.

Alex loved her overreaction. The joy it put on Josh's face, the ease it softened in his heart. He'd missed this camaraderie, the warmth of a partnership with a strong woman. But he couldn't risk fooling himself. Lisa's health issues were nothing to be taken lightly. He knew that. So why wouldn't this attraction abate? Why didn't the common sense of the situation send them both running?

"Lisa, we're done." Becky's voice trailed into the deepening night. "Can you braid my hair now?"

"Coming."

She stood and moved toward the house as if she belonged there, and Alex couldn't help but notice the way the evening shadows outlined the feminine curves of her lanky body, the easy stride of an accomplished woman, comfortable with herself.

He liked that about her. In truth, he liked a lot of things about her. The quick smile, her saucy demeanor, the quick repartee. She "got" him and that felt good.

Children's voices filled the air as he put away a few straggling toys before moving toward the house. Behind the laughter another voice stood out. Deeper. Crisper. Funny.

Lisa's womanly tone complemented the girls' higher pitch and Josh's tired whine. As he walked through the door, he noticed the kitchen first off. "Girls. Great job."

"Thanks, Dad." Emma glanced up from her book long enough to note his return, then buried herself in the extra wide chair once more.

"I did awesome, didn't I?" Becky preened at him from the breakfast barstool, her smiling face meeting his. She'd always needed that extra bit of reassurance, and sometimes tough love. When he saw her there, content, chores done, with Lisa braiding her long blond hair, his heart did a double take.

They presented a Dianne Dengel–type portrait in living color. Josh, flopped over a chair, tired, rumpled, close to losing it as the hour wore on. Emma, pristine in her fictional world, oblivious. Becky, soaking up the attention of the tall woman behind her...

And Lisa, smiling, chatting softly to Becky as her fingers made short work of some inside-out braiding maneuver Alex hadn't come close to mastering. He could tie any knot known to modern man, but braiding his daughter's long locks?

Not his forte.

"Isn't it pretty, Daddy?"

He smiled down at Becky, nodded and touched her chin with one finger. "Not pretty. Beautiful."

Becky glowed, pleased.

He lifted his gaze and let his eyes linger on Lisa until she glanced up. Paused. Her hands stilled, seeing his look. Reading the intent. "Absolutely beautiful," he said again. He held Lisa's attention until she caved under his scrutiny. Her fingers fumbled the last inches of hair. Her breathing accelerated.

If he had the right, he'd feather a kiss to her cheek right here and now. Whisper something in her ear.

But they'd set boundaries and while his heart seemed eager to steeplechase over those walls, his head knew better. But at this moment, he longed to follow his heart. See where it would lead.

"Daddy, do you miss Mommy?"

Josh's innocent words dashed cold water on growing feelings. *You're not in this alone. Think, man.* Alex didn't hesitate. "Every day."

"Me, too."

Josh yawned. He frowned and rubbed his eyes with fisted hands, a maneuver he'd done from the cradle.

Alex picked him up, had him say good-night, then carried the little fellow up the stairs. He did miss Jenny, although not having her there had become his new normal.

Josh's innocent query reminded him that three kids had lost their beloved mother. They'd grieved alongside him. He'd uprooted them and thrust them into a new town, a new setting, a new school. Kids could only be expected to handle so much. He'd changed their lives completely. That should be enough for the moment.

Lisa's laugh trailed up the stairs behind him, a response to Becky's quips.

Yeah, he missed the laughter and joy of a woman. But forging a relationship with Lisa meant putting his children in cancer's path again. Try as he might, he couldn't reconcile that insidious choice. Not on purpose.

When he came back downstairs, Lisa had tugged on a sweater, ready to leave. "Two things."

He tilted his head, inviting her to continue. She did. "This is from your mother-in-law."

"Nancy?"

"Nancy. Yes. I couldn't remember her name." She handed off the envelope to him. "She came by today and offered to help so I took her up on it. Nice woman. And she's great in the garden. Not afraid to get dirty. I love that about her."

Her words flummoxed Alex. Nancy had moved to an owner's association town house after Jenny's father died twelve years ago, but before that she'd had beautiful gardens in their east-side mansion-like home in an older section of Rochester. He'd forgotten about her penchant for gardening, and likely insulted her by not inviting her to help with Emma's project now that she was house-hunting here in Allegany County. He winced internally as another check went into the "strike" column of mother-in-law-relationship-building. "And?"

"If you take Becky's hair out in the morning, she'll have the crimped effect she wants. It will look kind of wild and untamed, but it's fun and the kids love it."

"You did all that just so I can take it out after she sleeps on it?" Alex sent a look of humor-filled disbelief toward the family room beyond. "Is that something?"

"It is if you're a girl."

He laughed and followed her to the door, wishing things were different. Wishing she didn't smell so good, even after working outside in the dirt. She proceeded through the door, letting the screen provide a natural barrier when she turned his way. "Thanks for letting me work with her, Alex."

He read the truth behind her words. She was grateful he'd moved beyond his initial reluctance. "I'm the one thanking you. You took what could have been a day of disappointment and filled it with hope for all three of them."

She lingered on the step for a short breath, eyed the starry sky, then drew her gaze back to his. "Good."

She left with a wave and a jangle of keys as she approached her car.

He wanted to stop her.

He couldn't.

He longed to explain why things had to be like this.

Except it made less sense as time went on.

Emma's voice drifted through the cooling night air, a chill reminder. Any decisions he made affected four people, not one. And his primary responsibility was to those children. Protecting them. Sheltering them. Nurturing them.

And that meant second-guessing his attraction to a beautiful woman who had to be declared off-limits. And that seemed plain wrong on multiple levels.

Chapter Seven

Lisa wanted to skip church on Mother's Day. Ignore God, faith and perfect-timing nonsense so she could work on her displays, displays that took half the time when her mother was alive.

But Maggie wasn't alive, and this was Lisa's first Mother's Day without her and she wanted to punch someone. Unfortunately, there were no candidates around except her father, and he'd been sucker-punched enough.

"Ready?" Her father held the door open.

He'd grayed more, she realized. And his face looked haggard. Fatigue lines etched deeper around eyes that used to gleam with warmth. The warmth was still there. She saw it when he played with Rosie. When he heard about Adam and Caroline's new pregnancy. When he chatted with a few of his farmer friends. But sadness and loss tempered the joy, like a shade, half-drawn. And Lisa didn't know how to help that.

"I am," she replied as she stepped through.

Morning sun greeted her. Mother's Day offered a mixed bag in the hills of western New York. Rain, sun and sometimes snow greeted the mid-May Sunday, but this year held promise. Warmth. Bright sun, a cloudless sky. She pasted a smile on her face, hoped it reached her eyes and accompanied her father.

They arrived, parked and walked into the gracious old stone church. The blended perfume of fresh spring blossoms wrapped itself around her and refused to let go.

Reverend Hannity's wife had tied ribbons of flowers to the ends of pews. Gorgeous potted blooms from Gardens & Greens ornamented the sanctuary, an explosion of donated color. The combination of scent and sight gentled her heart, and maybe her soul. Just a little.

Soft strains of organ music reminded her to gather with the choir. A part of her loved that call to music and worship, but today? Emotions threatened to topple her carefully constructed "I'm all right" persona. If that happened, the world would see through her thin facade of strength to the weak soul within.

Quiet, she kissed her father's cheek and moved to the choir loft, almost fearful. Would people want to hug her? Commiserate? Because she'd lose it if they did. And Lisa hated the thought of that. Breaking down. Falling apart. She'd held up through fire and brimstone already. She wasn't about to let a silly, made-up holiday ruin her track record.

"Good morning, Lisa." The choir director flashed her a quick smile.

"Lisa, hey. I've got your planner," Joan whispered. She handed it off as if today was any old day, and as Lisa moved to her spot, she realized her own foolishness.

These men and women understood her loss. They knew what it took to climb into the choir loft, heart-heavy and sad, lifting praise to God while questioning belief. Half the choir had lost someone to death or divorce in recent years. Parent. Sibling. Child.

She was a ninny, plain and simple. And when Alex and his family slipped into the church two minutes later through the side door, she chastised herself.

Maggie had been her mother for thirty-three years. Her parents had been married for over thirty-five years when Maggie died.

Alex's kids had barely gotten to know Jenny. And Josh didn't remember her at all, except through pictures.

She didn't dare look at Alex and those precious children, even though her spot in the choir offered a perfect vantage point. Banked emotions would surge upward, knowing what they'd endured throughout Jenny's fight. And after all that, they still had no choice but to tell their mother goodbye. What kind of God orchestrated that? What fairness could be discerned in Jenny's death? Perfect timing?

Uh-uh.

Emma turned, eyes up, searching for her. When she spotted Lisa, she waved. A smile brightened the little girl's face, a smile that lit the old church like a thousand flickering candles.

Alex turned, saw what Emma was doing and laid a quiet hand of caution on the girl's shoulder, but not before his gaze followed his daughter's.

His look mirrored her father's. Shaded. Gray. But then he met her eyes and smiled, and something in his look made her feel less alone. Less encumbered.

Which didn't make her hate Mother's Day any less, but gave her a short respite from yelling at God.

Alex situated himself squarely between Josh and Becky and hoped the two degrees of separation would keep them from squabbling during service. Becky had been bossing Josh around, Josh had been protesting in full vocal dissent and Emma had reamed out Becky for trying to run everyone's life, therefore ruining Sunday morning as usual.

Another happy day at the Steele house.

He'd put out fires as they popped up, but Alex Steele was nobody's fool. Either his methods were ineffective or he had the brattiest kids in the universe.

Unless their combined stress stemmed from

missing their mom and this made-up holiday struck an arrow into fragile little hearts, just like it did to his. Therefore he'd cut them some slack for the day.

"And before I let you go," the reverend finished, just shy of Alex's pew, "I want to take a moment to not only wish our mothers in attendance a happy Mother's Day..." His gentle gaze swept the congregation and he smiled. "But to remind you of the sacrifices mothers make. From days of old, mothers have shown us the way. In Kings, we saw the true mother's willingness to give up her child rather than see him divided. Sarah's faithful service was rewarded by a promised child in her later years. And who doesn't wish to have the strength of Moses' mother? Rather than see her baby killed, she set him afloat among the rushes where the king's daughter bathed, praying he'd be found and saved.

"So today," he continued, hands spread, "let's remember the example of strong mothers. Their faith, their resilience, their generous, giving spirits. Those with us, and those who've gone home to God."

Home to God.

Alex saw Emma mouth the three-word phrase, embracing the thought. Eyes moist, she glanced his way as though worried about him. Becky's chin quivered, then firmed, her tough-girl act firmly in place.

Josh climbed onto Alex's lap.

Had he understood the pastor's words? Did it mean much at four years old?

Josh laid his buzzed blond head against Alex's chest and whispered, "I miss my Mommy."

Alex choked. His gut rose up. His heart went thick. Tight.

For a few seconds he struggled to breathe.

He made the decision then and there to keep them busy, so busy that they wouldn't have time to think about what day it was. What they'd lost over two years ago. How empty their old house seemed without Jenny's smile, her laugh, her spirited presence.

He ushered them out the side door before the final hymn ended, got them into the car and aimed for home before the crush of people put three motherless kids into a sympathetic situation they might not be able to handle.

And even if they could? He knew he couldn't.

"Lisa?"

Alyssa Michaels's voice stopped Lisa as she tried unsuccessfully to edge out the back door, avoiding as many people as possible. Because she loved her second-cousin, she paused and turned. "Alyssa. Hey. Happy Mother's Day."

"Thank you." Alyssa scrambled as her youngest son, Clay, tried to escape her hand and head to the playground across the Park Round. Sunday traffic ran expectedly slow, but cars and little boys didn't mix, even in slow mode. "In a minute, kid. Say hi to Lisa and let Mommy talk."

A firm lip protruded from beneath Clay's stubborn gaze. Monkey bars and swings held more allure than distant cousins, it seemed.

Alyssa sent him a sour look, but was saved from Mother's Day discipline by a pair of strong, fatherly arms. "I'll take him over," Trent told her. He flashed Lisa a quick smile. "You guys talk about the Fourth."

"The Fourth?" Lisa walked down the steps, away from the crowded church doors. "Fill me in."

"We're doing a family picnic at our place after the parade and memorial blessing."

"Sounds great." Lisa withdrew her phone and tapped in a quick reminder. "What can I bring?"

"Your whole family, for starters. I'll send out an email invite and make it a Facebook event, but people like your dad won't see that."

Lisa grinned. Her father's lack of techno savvy was renowned. "I'll tell them. How about if I do a pasta salad—"

"Your pasta salad is Trent's all-time favorite," Alyssa chimed in.

Lisa smiled. "And Caro loves to make that fluffy Jell-O and fruit thing. With the marshmallows."

"Jaden's favorite. With two happy men in my life, life as we know it can continue. I'm having a few close neighbors, too."

Warning bells exploded like Independence Day fireworks in Lisa's brain.

"Most of them have their own thing to do, but a few of them don't have family here," Alyssa continued.

The internal fireworks kaboomed in a blast of thunder. "Like?"

Alyssa waved a hand as if the conversation was over. "Whoever's available."

"Alyssa…"

"Gotta go. The restaurant will be crazy today and I ducked out for services. We're celebrating tonight at home. Quiet. Peaceful. Knowing my husband, it's most likely going to be pizza. And hey," Alyssa reached out and grabbed Lisa in a big hug, then backed off quickly. "I know today isn't easy for you, so I'm not saying anything about it, but I'm always here for you. You know that, right? No matter what happens. Ever."

Her pledge went deeper than surface words. Lisa knew that. Alyssa's mother had been a solid rock supporter during Maggie's illness and passing. Susan Langley had organized the ladies from various churches to bring meals. Volunteers had helped run the Christmas tree sales lot as Maggie's condition worsened. Susan and Alyssa would have her back, she knew, if the unthinkable happened and she had a recurrence. She'd spent the last hour praying for that not to happen, but she'd learned the hard way that not all prayers are answered.

She'd prayed for Evan to conquer his fears. He'd run scared and never looked back.

She'd prayed for her mother's recovery. Didn't happen.

Therefore she'd decided God was way too picky for her liking these days. End of discussion.

She waved Alyssa off, but saw the bright light in her cousin's eyes. The quick smile that said Alex and those cute kids might be hanging around at the family Fourth of July shindig.

A twinge hit her, mid-section. Not knife-like, not horrid, just a spreading ache, another reminder that everyday aches and pains take on new meaning for cancer survivors. Her first year post-treatment, she'd been certifiably paranoid. Every twinge, each sore spot, muscle ache...

She'd had them all checked, and each time she was fine. She knew statistically that if her cancer metastasized, it probably would have happened by now. But by numeric standards she never should have gotten the disease in the first place, so statistics didn't mean all that much.

Mentally, every abdominal twinge had her revisiting the warning label on her prescription. *"Heightened risk of uterine cancer."*

You're obsessing. Being absurd. Knock it off.

The internal scolding sounded a lot like her mother, but she couldn't think about Maggie today. Not with a busy store, people stopping throughout the day to buy their mothers plants and flowers.

Five months gone was way too soon to think about their loss, about no more Mother's Day celebrations late in the evening once sales calmed down. She'd ignore the reason for the day, because otherwise she'd lose it.

Monday morning Alex congratulated himself. He'd made it through another Mother's Day. He'd sent his mother flowers, did the same for Nancy and pretended he didn't get emotional when she called to thank him for his thoughtfulness.

He knew better. He wasn't being thoughtful, he was being thorough, and that shamed him. He'd taken the kids to the Kirkwood Lake playground after church, then a movie, ordered takeout from the local Chinese restaurant and pretended there was no holiday from the early morning church bell call to worship until the sun sank low on the horizon late that evening.

They'd gotten through, again. And some days that was all he asked of God.

He pulled his car into the driveway just west of the Fitzgeralds' farm access drive along the northern boundary of the Fitzgeralds' farm. He walked up to the door and knocked.

No answer.

He searched for a bell.

No doorbell.

He knocked again.

The metallic click of a gun release dropped him to his knees.

Why hadn't he brought Samson along? Why did he keep underestimating the level of crime and criminals in this sweet rural town that hid so much behind white ruffled curtains? What in Sam Hill was he thinking, that life down here would be sweet? Simple? Good?

A phone rang. Not his.

He called for backup, crouched low, out of sight from the windows. "Unknown party has drawn a gun on an officer, 1212 County Road Seven, I repeat, 1212 County Road Seven, request backup!"

"Boss, why are you botherin' Miss Mavis?"

Iuppa's voice answered him and sounded genuinely perplexed. He'd be more confused when Alex put a warning letter in his work folder later. Or killed him. That might be the better option, overall.

"She can't shoot you, boss."

Irritation spiked Alex's temper. "Iuppa, shut up and get me backup."

"Backup's on the way, but right about now Miss Mavis will be opening the door because Byron Bradley and his wife watch out for her. If someone comes to her door, they call her to tell her if it's okay to open it. After she makes like she's loading a shotgun, of course."

"It's fake."

"The gun's real enough," Iuppa explained, and Alex envisioned the smirk on the local investigator's face because it came through plain as day in his voice. "But not loaded. Miss Mavis is—"

Blind.

Alex didn't need Sal to explain further as the old woman swung the door wide. "You the new fella at the station house?"

Alex put an internal stop on his adrenaline-fed heart and nodded. "Yes, ma'am."

"Sorry about that." She waved toward a shotgun slung across the honey maple tabletop behind her. "I keep it to discourage salesmen. Once folks know a blind woman lives here, no tellin' what they might do, you know."

Alex couldn't deny it. And because Mavis was clearly well into her golden years, her methodology proved successful. "Whatever works, ma'am. It's not loaded, right?"

"Never." She smiled and pushed the screen door open for him. "Come in, take a seat. I expect you're here about that nasty business next door."

Next door? The Fitzgerald farm was an easy half-mile away, but in the country...

"At the Fitzgeralds' place." She waved a hand east.

"Yes."

The sound of far-off sirens pulled his attention. Surely Iuppa had canceled the backup request. Hadn't he?

"Their tractor path lines right up with the morning sun side of my sleeping room," Miss Mavis continued as the sirens grew closer. Louder. She pointed left and Alex took a couple of steps that way. A tidy room lay in the back corner of the house, with two windows. One east. One south. Perfect for hearing equipment going in and out of Lisa's back entry.

"Did you hear anything the night they were robbed, Ms. Anderson?"

"I surely did." She sat in a chair alongside the small dinette table, and Alex followed suit, just her, him and a 16-gauge black walnut-trimmed Ithaca Deerslayer hanging out together.

He fought a sigh as the sirens screamed closer, but knew Iuppa followed the letter of the law. He hadn't requested the backup canceled and Iuppa was aching to show him up. Let him know that a local appointee would have better served the needs of the area.

Which meant Alex better put a smile on his face, so he did. He turned to Miss Mavis as he stood. "Sorry. I heard the gun and called for backup. They think they're saving me. I'll call them off and we can talk."

"I'da put my good pearls on if I'd known I was gonna enjoy so much company!" the old woman joked.

She defined endearing in blue cotton floral, the calf-length dress retro and sweet. Her snow-white hair was twisted and pinned up in the back. Her sightless eyes gleamed.

Alex laughed, remembering she couldn't see his quiet smile. "They'll get a good chuckle at the station, Miss Mavis." He keyed his radio, gave the order to stand down and went through the screen door.

Six troopers and two sheriff's deputies armed with nothing more than "gotcha!" grins met his gaze from the driveway. He stopped on the step and stared them down until the smiles began to fade and concern flickered in. When he hoped they'd squirmed enough, he waved his hand. "Back to work, gentlemen. Fun's over."

The grins returned, and despite the fact that Iuppa had done this deliberately, it worked out all right. He'd passed a test with these officers today— he saw it in their smiles of acceptance when he waved them off.

He returned to Mavis, took her information at a country snail's pace, ate two of Brenda Bradley's homemade sugar cookies, declared them incomparable and aimed his car back toward the station house an hour later.

He'd made a friend in Miss Mavis. In all fairness, those cookies *were* the best he'd ever had, and he found out the truck and trailer that exited from the back access lane to the Fitzgeralds' place headed west on the two-lane road, away from the Interstate.

That little bit of information put a different spin on things. The thief wasn't looking to go far, or be recognized by early patrols on I-86. He or she was looking to blend into the country landscape. Unfortunately for Alex, they'd been successful.

Lisa's fingers hovered over the keyboard as her eyes claimed one email.

From Alex.

She put her heart on cruise control and opened the message. "Becky and Emma would like to enroll in your June gardening/nature class. Is there still room?"

On the roster, yes.

In her heart, no.

She sighed, ground her teeth, then hit Reply. "Yes. I'm attaching the form. You can fill it out and email it back to me. Lisa."

She hesitated, scoured the abbreviated note for hidden messages, found none and hit Send.

The phone rang twelve seconds later. She knew that because she was watching the clock and when "Private Caller" came up in her phone, she knew it was most likely Alex and answered anyway. "Gardens & Greens, Lisa speaking, how may I help you?"

"It's Alex."

Clearly her take-this-slow cruise control function was deficient because her pulse ramped up to race-car time. "Hey. What's up?" She clamped down her internal reaction and kept her voice careful and casual.

"I got your email."

"The one I sent twenty-seven seconds ago?"

He laughed and the deep, warm tones softened her hard-line stand. "That's the one. I know I'll see you tomorrow…"

"For Emma's project." She inserted that to remind him of the whys and wherefores.

"Yes. But I also wanted to fill you in on the progress of our investigation."

"Lt. Samson called me. He explained there was nothing new to report, but said you're working on it."

"Exactly. Although we do know the guy headed west with the loaded trailer, but no end location as yet." Alex paused a moment before he added, "I know it's a tough go when you don't have the proper equipment around."

It was. Lisa considered his words, then shrugged. "We're making do. One of the farmers let us borrow his mower. That's a huge help in keeping the grounds up. The small tractor is cumbersome but we're managing."

"I'm sure you are." His voice deepened. "But I know it's not easy and I don't want you to think I've forgotten about you. I mean it, the theft. The equipment."

He half stuttered that last and another corner of Lisa's heart melted like chocolate in sunlight, which meant she better stay in the cool shade of resistance. "Thank you. I'll see you tomorrow. Four o'clock still okay?"

"Fine."

He sounded like he didn't want to stop the conversation. Neither did Lisa. But she saw no benefit in drawing things out. They both understood the boundaries.

But hearing his voice, trying to read between the lines? That was the stuff teen novels were made of, and Lisa didn't have time for make-believe. Not when reality tugged at her twenty-four-seven.

The phone rang again. She answered, then flashed a smile as she crossed to the outside door. "Sabrina. Hey. How's everything?"

"Better."

"Good!" Lisa stamped emphasis on the single word. Sabrina had been diagnosed with breast cancer two weeks before and followed the path most patients embraced. First you cry. Then you fight. She'd found Lisa through an online breast cancer site that linked patients with survivors.

"You've met with your never-ending team of doctors?"

"My head is spinning."

"I know." Lisa remembered all too well. "And you're calling with questions, right?"

"Yes, but I hate bothering you," the other woman replied. "I know you're open about what happened to you, but I feel like I'm intruding in your personal life."

Her words broadsided Lisa. If Sabrina felt that

way and still made the call, how many women hesitated and didn't dial her number?

Many, she realized, and that inspired a flash of insight. Breast cancer patients needed a group. A corps. A legion of survivors, willing to talk. "You're not intruding," she reassured the newly diagnosed woman. "But I think we should start a group similar to the Breast Cancer Coalitions that bigger cities have. What do you think? If we band together to share info and support each other, that would be great, wouldn't it?"

"That would be wonderful." Sabrina's voice hitched. "I would love a respite where my cancer doesn't put deadly fear on everyone's face."

Lisa had lived with that expression on Evan's face for months. He'd distanced himself from her as if her cancer were contagious. As if she was doomed. His negativity made it hard to stay in the positive zone she needed during long days of chemo and surgical recovery. She would have loved to be connected to someone upbeat and positive. Someone who had walked the walk. "Sabrina Addison, I am formally issuing you an invitation to join the Southern Tier Breast Cancer Corps, a community of women aimed at uplifting and informing breast cancer patients."

"This is a brand-new group and you've already come up with a name?" Sabrina remarked. "Sweet."

Lisa laughed. "I'll send out an email to a bunch

of local gals and we'll see if we can get this off the ground, but you're first, Sabrina. You want in?"

"You bet I do." Sabrina's voice rose with hope. "When is our first meeting?"

Lisa mentally scanned her calendar. "I've got this Tuesday evening free. Let's start with that. We can meet at the farmhouse."

"I'll bring brownies," Sabrina declared. "With chocolate fudge frosting."

Chocolate, faith and her stubborn nature had helped Lisa through a lot of cancer valleys, although the faith faction had taken a number of hits. She'd attended a winter/spring Bible study session called "Why Bad Things Happen to Good People" and left the course not one bit smarter than when she started, but her "show me" attitude might have had something to do with that. "You do that," she told Sabrina. "I'll see you Tuesday at seven."

"Thanks, Lisa."

The tremor in Sabrina's voice brought back a lot of memories. Lisa headed into the garden area, determined to make a difference any way she could. "None needed. See you Tuesday."

"Lisa's coming!" Becky screeched the alert from her second-story-high tree perch in the backyard. "Josh, don't hog her!"

"She's my friend, too." Josh aimed a sour look at Becky, a face that invited pure chaos and sibling fighting.

Not today, Alex decided. "Josh, can you help me carry these pots to the other side of the house?"

"Sure!" The little guy raced to Alex's side, tried to hoist a one-gallon potted hosta and groaned. The heavy pot listed, tipping Josh sideways.

"Whoa, there, partner. Try this one." Alex handed him a tray of waxed begonias. "Better?"

"Yes." Josh pulled his shoulders up, proud. "It's big but not as heavy."

"All about balance, my boy." He lifted his gaze as Lisa exited her car. Cargo shorts on great legs. A fitted T-shirt with the Gardens & Greens logo. A baseball cap to keep the sun out of her eyes, and when he drew closer he noted the familiar pinstripes. "A Yankees fan."

"Like there's another choice?" She pretended surprise. "Almost thirty world championships do some serious talking, Alex."

"And humble about it, too." As Josh bent to set the tray of plants on the ground, Alex called out, "Hey, buddy, turn around. Let Lisa see your shirt."

Josh turned and proudly pointed to the New York Yankees emblem across the front of his gray T-shirt.

Alex shoulder-nudged Lisa. "You're among friends here."

Josh noticed Lisa's cap, screeched and raced for them. "You love the Yankees, Lisa? Me, too! I'm going to be a shortstop when I grow up, just like Jeter!"

Lisa bent and arched the little boy a look of understanding. "Jeter rocks, doesn't he?"

"Oh, yeah!" Josh assumed a batter's stance, then did the renowned Jeter-move of touching the brim of his cap, holding up his balancing arm, digging his toes into the batter's box sand and facing the pitcher, nonchalant. "I love Jeter."

"Me, too." Lisa's grin said she admired everything about the Yankee shortstop, and Alex felt a crushing need to stand taller and change the subject. Competing with a baseball icon didn't make his short list. *You're not competing with anything*, his conscience reminded him. *She's off-limits, remember?*

His pledge was easier to remember when Lisa was in the abstract. Here? In person? With Yankee-blue toenails peeking from the tips of her sandals? His promise bordered on impossible. "Yankee toes?"

She glanced down and slanted him a bright smile as the girls came charging from the backyard. "Awesome, right?" She wiggled her toes for effect and even Josh marveled. "I used a white undercoat, then a navy blue shatter topcoat. When it splits, I get the Yankee blue-and-white effect. Pretty cool."

"Lisa." Emma ground to a halt and bent to inspect her mentor's toes. "We love the Yankees."

"So I hear."

"Can you do that to me?"

"And me?" Becky echoed.

"And—"

"Not a chance, bud." Alex lifted the little boy and pointed down. "Girls do nails. Not boys."

"But…"

"No buts."

"Big league catchers get their nails done," Lisa reminded him as she clasped the girls' hands, winked their way and moved toward the house. "Otherwise the pitchers might miss the signs."

"Not all of 'em, and not my kid." Alex angled her a mock frown that bordered a scowl.

Her smile broadened. "All right, macho man. I see everything got delivered this morning."

"Lisa, it's amazing." Emma indicated the house with a sweep of her hand. "We got the delivery, then Dad had us split everything up and carry it to the right side of the house based on our drawings. That way we don't waste your time this afternoon."

"How thoughtful." A flash of insecurity darkened Lisa's eyes, enough to make Alex move closer. He didn't want her to assume they wanted to be rid of her sooner. "Actually…I was hoping you'd have time to stay for supper when we're done. We're ordering pizza and wings because I figured this would take a while."

"It will, but supper…" Lisa glanced away from him, obviously reluctant. When he reached one finger to her chin, lifting it his way, she gave in. "Sure."

A funny ache welled inside Alex. The feel of her

skin beneath his finger. The look of longing in her eyes, the glimpse of regret by what couldn't be, and suddenly he wanted nothing more than to make joy a constant in her life.

And his.

The touch of her skin made him want to lean in. Kiss her. Feel her mouth beneath his. Sample the loving, giving beauty that marked Lisa as special beyond words.

But he couldn't for more reasons than should be humanly possible.

She broke the spell by stepping away. That was a good thing.

But it didn't feel good, it felt like he'd just lost the cell phone signal on a very important phone call.

Patience. Perseverance. Time.

He wasn't as patient as he should be. And he hated unfilled time, but he knew the cost of rushing things, and the possible ramifications of falling for a cancer survivor. He'd studied the odds of recurrence, trying to think of ways to keep Jenny from getting sick again.

That was before he realized the choice was already out of his hands. He choked back a sigh, or maybe a growl. Either way, swallowing the emotion tightened his chest. His heart.

"How about Emma and I work here, with Josh helping us?" Lisa turned a bright smile toward the kids and held out her hands for a shovel. "You and Becky tackle the front. That way we're close enough to talk and ask questions, but not so close we trip over each other."

He heard three words. "Not so close."

He hated the hidden message, even though it was exactly what he'd asked for.

Was he being scared or sensible? He didn't know. And until he did, he'd be smart to follow her lead and back off. "All right, Beck, you're with me."

Lisa staved Becky's protest by adding, "We'll switch up later. Becky and I will work together on the west side, while you guys do the back."

"Okay!" Becky's grin made the gap in her front teeth look wider. She grabbed Alex's hand in a pleasant show of solidarity, a welcome change. "Let's go, Dad. Maybe we can beat them."

"Competitive."

Alex met Lisa's look with measured resignation. "Inherent, I guess."

She laughed, sat on the stoop and changed her sandals for scuffed-up garden sneakers. "Can't be ruining my new toes, right?"

"Right."

She sent him a teasing look from the top step, and something in that humor-filled gaze made him more aware of Lisa, the woman. Resilient. Faithful. Beautiful. Funny.

And the khaki shorts that nipped to a narrow waist weren't anything a man should ignore.

"Work time."

"Yes."

With effort he pulled his head out of what could be and set to work with Becky.

"Pizza's here!"

"Let's scrub up, gang," Lisa commanded. They'd gotten a lot done, and the few remaining plants could be set in the shade and planted tomorrow. "Should we put the shovels away or leave them out so you guys can finish up after church?"

"Set them here, by the house," Alex called from the back door. "And if you guys split bathrooms, you can be washed up and ready for food in five."

"Just enough time for the pizza to cool off and be edible," Lisa assured the kids. She followed them into the house. They scrambled for various wash-up areas, and she smiled as Josh dragged a step stool to the laundry room. The little fellow began scrubbing garden soil and leftover chocolate chip cookie smudges from his hands with more gusto than soap while Lisa moved toward the kitchen sink.

"Garden soil is non-toxic, right?" Alex made the observation close to her ear, so close, in fact, that when she turned her head his way, he was there. Right there. And the natural thing to do when a heart-interest's lips were that close was to kiss them. Even when they were forbidden territory.

So she did.

And he kissed her back in a kiss that felt like everything good and holy and wonderful in the world just righted itself in the doorway of that sweet old kitchen. The scent of him, garden-rich, woodsy. Earthy. Rugged. Male.

The grip of his hands as they slipped around her, drawing her closer, tucking her alongside his heart.

She didn't want the kiss to end.

Alex appeared to be of the same mindset and seconds stretched into long moments, but when the clatter of feet pounded down the stairs, he released her and withdrew, without looking apologetic or regretful.

The man looked pleased, as if the kiss was everything he hoped it would be. Lisa tried to step back, but Alex grabbed her hand and drew her further into the kitchen. "No, you don't. There's no escaping now, Lisa."

She swung her gaze to his, and he smiled, teasing. "Not before food, at least."

"Alex, I—"

"Spare us the common-sense reasoning for the moment, okay?" He stood dead-set in front of her and held her gaze. "I get it. We both do. But I've been wanting to kiss you for days, possibly weeks, and I'm not going to pretend it wasn't an eleven on a one-to-ten scale, so let's leave it at that for the moment. Plain cheese?" He tipped his attention toward the twin boxes on the table. "Or loaded?"

"Loaded."

"That's my girl." He grinned, touched the tip of her nose with his finger and turned as the girls hurried in.

"Dad, can we eat in the family room and watch the gymnastics competition?"

"Yes."

"Me, too?" asked Josh.

"Not until your ape-like tendencies improve, kid. Eating in the family room doesn't include wiping your hands on the carpet. Or your pants." He put a slice of cheese pizza on the table, then held out Josh's chair. "On top of that, your sisters could use a break."

"From me?"

"From everything." Alex's answer employed sibling diplomacy. "And this way you get Lisa all to yourself."

"Oh, that's right!" Josh shot a look of excitement her way, and Lisa's internal turmoil rumbled upward again. The little guy's contagious joy tugged her further into the heart of this family but his emotional well-being was the very reason she and Alex couldn't reach for the dream.

The house phone interrupted them. Alex left her and Josh to say grace while he took the call. When he came back into the room, he looked distressed. "Lisa, I've got to go. I'll call and see if my Saturday babysitter can come watch the kids."

"Can't Grandma come?" Josh wondered.

Alex's hand paused over the phone. He eyed the boy, then nodded. "Grandma's closer now, so she might like that. I'll ask, Josh." He hit a number, waited, then said, "Nancy, I just got called into work. Is there any chance you're available to watch the kids for the night?"

Lisa noted the initial reluctance in his eyes as he placed the call. But he called, and that meant he was willing to work through things, right? The friction between Alex and his former mother-in-law might not concern her, but family feuds weren't her style. She wanted the same to be true for Alex.

"Fifteen minutes? Perfect. Lisa's here—we were continuing Emma's project today, so if she can stay—?" He raised a look of question her way.

Lisa nodded.

"Then I'll take off and come back when I can." He paused, listening to her answer, then hung up the phone. "She's on her way," he told Lisa. "You're all right hanging out until she gets here?"

"Fine. Yes. Go."

He sent her a look of gratitude as he grabbed the realities of his job from a locked high cupboard. Badge. ID. Gun.

The last made her realize how a huge part of Alex's life dealt with danger. Funny, she hadn't thought of that until now. Maybe because he wore street clothes? And worked from the office? Because she thought of that constantly with Adam. Seeing her brother in uniform, she prayed for his safety.

Reality hit her as she watched Alex kiss the kids goodbye and move her way. Like Adam, this guy faced danger in his daily life. And these kids had already lost one parent. Were they playing fair with anyone's heart by taking the brakes off and seeing where this attraction might lead? No.

"Hey. Thanks."

He didn't say more than that, but his eyes said plenty. Regret, humor and a heightened sense of camaraderie blended into an almost wistful smile. "For the gardening help? You're welcome."

He grazed her chin with the palm of his hand in a caress so sweet and gentle it made her eyes moisten. "That, too." He read her look, saw the swim of emotions and his smile mingled with regret. "Gotta go."

"Yes. Go. Bye."

He may have left reluctantly, but he ran to the car, and Lisa saw another quality to admire in Alex Steele: he had his troops' back, all day, every day. He wasn't just an officer. He was a leader, and that quality drew her close even while she should be pushing away.

Wait on the Lord...

Old words, ancient wisdom, a song of the ages, but Lisa had no desire to tempt fate. Not at the expense of those children's well-being. She'd witnessed the outcome of what happened when adults forgot to put children first. These days it was almost epidemic because of careless adult behavior. How could she knowingly chance that with kids who had already lost one mother?

She couldn't. Wouldn't. Although that sweet kiss

tempted her forward, which meant she had to re-gather her reserve and step back.

You never used to fear anything, her conscience scoffed. *And you used to believe in God, the Father Almighty. Is this what it's come to? It's easy to have faith when everything's going right, but it's more important to have faith when the world tumbles down around you. What is wrong with you?*

Lisa hushed the curt reminder. She'd embraced her faith fully for decades, but now...

Where was God when she needed Him? When she prayed for Evan to be stronger? To stay with her?

When she prayed for her mother's return to health? Exactly where had prayer gotten her? Zero plus zero equals a big, fat nothing.

So that's your new normal? Lack of trust? Thin faith? Doesn't the Bible chat it up about that pretty regularly?

Lisa ignored the mental reprimand, stowed the leftover pizza in the fridge and went into the family room to play with the kids until Nancy arrived.

Did every little twinge make her nervous and scared inside?

Yes. And she had every right to be, thank you very much.

"I'm here." Nancy's voice called out from the back door entry.

Lisa tried to untangle herself from the jumble

of body parts snuggling close to her on the worn, comfy family room sectional. She discovered that when Josh and Becky held tight, escape proved nearly impossible, so Nancy found them wrestling as she let herself in.

"Grandma!"

"Hey, Grandma, you're here. Why did you come?" Emma asked the question innocently, but her words sent a short flash of pain to Nancy's eyes.

"Daddy called me because he had to go in to work."

"Couldn't Lisa stay?"

Nancy's lips pressed together. She raised her eyes to Lisa's, speculation in her gaze. "You'd have to ask Lisa that question."

Lisa raised her hands in surrender. "Hey, I'm the hired help, kid. I came to get down and dirty in the garden with you guys. Mission accomplished. Now I must go," she tried to disengage herself from Josh, but discovered that four-year-olds were more octopus-oriented than she ever would have thought. As she loosened one of his grips, another foot or hand wrapped around her. Finally she hoisted him, tipped him upside down and held him there for several seconds while he giggled, squirming with delight. "I will let you down if you promise to say goodbye politely. It's either that, or off to bed. Your choice."

Josh huffed a breath and capitulated. "All right."

Lisa righted the little boy and he gave her one last hug. "I just don't want you to go."

Her heart opened a little wider to the wealth of possibilities under this roof. Alex's gaze, his kiss, the feel of his arms wrapped around her...

Oh, she could welcome those arms the rest of her life.

"Josh, she has to go," Becky cut in sharply. "She doesn't live here."

Cool awareness dawned. Lisa stepped back. "Becky's right. I've got to get some things done for tomorrow. This is a crazy busy time at our farm."

"Thanks for helping Emma today." Nancy's words came with thin warmth, and the breast cancer ribbon she wore on her collar reminded Lisa of what this woman had lost. Lisa's presence in Alex's home probably drummed up a plethora of mixed emotions. That was the last thing she wanted to do.

"My pleasure." Lisa grasped Nancy's hand. "You told me you love gardening, right?"

Nancy nodded, tentative.

"Well I'm tied up for the next several days and we're due for a hot streak. Can you help these guys spread mulch around the sides of the house after they finish planting tomorrow?"

"Grandma, could you?" Emma's face lit up at the thought of her grandmother's help. Her shining smile softened Nancy's features.

"I'd love to."

"Thanks." Lisa kept it simple, because a grandmother's love for her grandchildren should be uncomplicated. She'd seen that with her mother and

Rosie. Nancy deserved the same kind of open-door policy. And if Alex had to work through the night, he'd most likely welcome adult help tomorrow. She hoped.

She said a quick goodbye, climbed into her SUV and headed for the outskirts of town. Alone, she couldn't get her mind past the kiss, the press of Alex's mouth on hers, the utterly safe feeling of being wrapped in the officer's arms. She could honestly say she'd never felt like that with Evan.

Alex had trusted and prayed and fought the good fight and lost the war.

Evan had given up, turned his back and run.

Alex's wife had died.

Lisa had lived.

Lisa couldn't see the rationale in either scenario. Who made these decisions? God? Inexplicable destiny? Genetic branding from the moment of conception?

She'd prayed to live and she did. But every day people prayed the same prayer and lost their lives. Young people. Old people. Babies. Why?

No answers came. She'd grown up believing in God's perfect timing, but had a hard time rationalizing what had happened to Alex. To her mother.

Pain washed over her, piercing. Knife-like.

She missed her mother. Maggie's constant cheer had bolstered her through so much.

And now she'd kissed Alex Steele, a mind-bending, soul-searching kiss that opened a wealth of possibilities. Now that she knew what she'd been missing, keeping her distance would only prove harder.

He'd kissed Lisa Fitzgerald. Thoroughly. Convincingly.

And he intended to do it again.

But first Alex needed to catch some sleep and be grateful tonight's standoff had ended without incident. Their negotiator had done an admirable job of defusing the guy with a gun, and Alex would put a note of commendation in her folder on Monday.

But today's schedule embraced sleep, church, gardening and... He tried but couldn't come up with a reason to draw Lisa over to the house on what would be a frantically busy Sunday at the garden center.

You need a reason? After that kiss?

It was an excellent kiss, he admitted to himself, and being a purposeful man he figured he might be able to tempt her over with the promise of another. The allure of that would work for him, hands down.

Women are different.

Oh, he got that. Which meant he needed a battle strategy. A plan. And Alex hadn't climbed the ladder of the New York State Troopers without a step-by-step process laid out years ago.

Finding her farm equipment might help gain you serious points.

The mental reminder smacked him as he pulled

into the driveway. They'd had no further leads in the case, and each day made a quiet theft harder to solve. Dark of night, no witnesses, and precious little evidence other than flattened grass, an oil smear and a part of a tractor tire tread. Not enough of anything to steer the investigation in a solid direction despite the information he'd gleaned from Miss Mavis.

Sensor lights flooded the front yard as he walked to the side door and let himself into a clean house. Short weeks ago Nancy's help would have insulted him.

Today, after spending the day at the station, the evening working outside with Lisa and the kids, and the rush to a dangerous intervention on a little side street in Cuba, New York, he was grateful to see the clean countertops. A crumb-less table. Toys put away in the family room. Laundry neatly folded in a white plastic basket.

Nancy tiptoed toward him from the living room. "A long night."

A few weeks back he'd have hunted for censure in her tone.

Not tonight. Maybe he was maturing. Or adjusting. Or just plain accepting the fact that he didn't have to be Super Dad or anything more than he was. Accepting that might give him time to breathe. "Yeah. Thank you for straightening up."

"I commandeered the children."

The image made him smile. "I've been trying to do better with that myself."

Nancy's expression agreed. "I think losing Jenny made me feel like I needed to spoil them to protect them. Now I realize I was acting on emotion, not instinct. Because Jenny would have laughed at that notion."

"Yes." Alex gestured toward the extra bedroom. "You're welcome to stay. It's late to head back to the condo."

She considered his offer before she moved toward the door. "No, I'll go back for the night. But I promised Lisa I'd help the kids mulch the gardens tomorrow afternoon. If that's all right?"

"I'd be grateful." Alex held the door open for her. "And have supper here with us. We'll make it family dinner Sunday."

Her eyes brightened. Her smile went wide, and Alex kicked himself internally. Why had he let things get out of hand with his mother-in-law? She was a good person, he knew that. Yet he'd let walls spring up between them. Time to pull out the sledgehammer and knock them down to size.

"I'll make lasagna."

Nancy's mouthwatering lasagna had been a Sunday tradition before Jenny got sick. Now it could become a new custom, here, in Allegany County. "Perfect."

He went upstairs, less tired than he thought he'd be, and more at peace than he'd been in years.

Chapter Eight

Lisa balanced a tray of cupcakes and cookies while Sabrina followed with a hot water carafe on Tuesday evening. "Amy, can you shift the stuff off that table, please?"

"Sure." Amy Jankowski moved stacks of papers to the old oak sideboard, then scooped up a pile of gardening catalogs. "Busy these days?"

"I knew you guys wouldn't care if straightening up the living room didn't make my to-do list," Lisa confessed. "This time of year I'm lucky to be in the house at all. Dad keeps suggesting a housekeeper, but that seems awkward."

Amy glanced around and hiked a brow of disbelief. "Like this isn't?"

"I know," Lisa admitted, making a face. "A part of me would feel better if everything was in its place like when Mom was here. Another part doesn't want anyone touching our stuff. Which is silly because I hate the clutter."

"My sister does housecleaning for people and businesses." Sabrina addressed Lisa but her gaze included the whole group. "And when you're sick, it's easy to let stupid things weigh on you. Like dust bunnies under the beds and bathrooms that need scrubbing but you're too sick to care."

"Or down in the dumps," a middle-aged woman added. Her comment drew a communal nod.

"My nemesis is organizing the kids' clothing," one young mother confessed. She reached up to adjust the thin knit hat covering her bald head. "We've had two changes of seasons between my chemo and surgery and I have piles of clothing everywhere. Wrong sizes, wrong seasons, wrong kid. It's driving me crazy," she admitted. "If your sister is available to help with stuff like that, I'd hire her in a heartbeat."

"And if anyone is tight on money and doesn't mind an old lady volunteering, I'm available." Viola Mannington reached for the carafe and offered to pour for others with a tilt of her head. "I can't get up and down in folks' gardens the way my sister Twila can, but I can clean and organize inside as good as ever. Well." She angled them a sweet old lady smile and lifted one shoulder. "Almost."

The gathered women returned her smile. Viola was a three-decade survivor and, other than a mild case of lymphedema swelling in her left arm, the stout woman had done well. Her milestones offered hope to the newly diagnosed.

Lisa perched on the sofa arm and surveyed the room. "Before we do anything else, I want to thank you all for coming tonight, especially on such short notice."

"Well, it makes sense to start a group," Viola cut in from the sideboard. "Shoulda done this long ago, but now's as good a time as any."

A murmur of consent rounded the circle of eleven women, all breast cancer patients or survivors. The fact that six of the women were under age forty wasn't lost on anyone.

Lisa nodded. "We can do this formally or not, our choice. There are pros and cons to both, but I think it's easier to get the word out to other patients and survivors if we formalize the group. What do—"

The doorbell cut her off. She rose to answer it, but Caro came through the kitchen arch. "I'm about to bathe a really messy kid before taking her home. I'll let them in, ladies."

She waved to the group as she cut through the living room. Short seconds later she reappeared, with Alex close behind.

Alex.

Here.

Now.

His eyes caught Lisa's as Caro headed back to Rosie in the kitchen. His smile went wide, engaging. Contagious. And then he glanced around.

Realization stole the grin. His gaze shaded as

he took in the circle of women. Chemo hats. Pink shirts. Bandannas. Pink ribbons.

And Caro had made pink-frosted cupcakes, glistening with white sparkling sugar and rose-toned sprinkles.

"Alex." Lisa rose, determined to bridge the moment, someway, somehow. "Do you have news about the equipment?"

A true cop, he regained his composure in a heartbeat, but she saw. She knew. Faced with this stupid disease, he'd cringed and Lisa had faced that look too often with Evan. At least this time, she recognized the symptoms. Once bitten, twice shy. She waggled a Yankee-pinstriped pink baseball cap at him. "How cool that I can support two causes at once?"

He noted the cap with a smile, but it was a faint imitation of the eye-catching grin he'd given her the past weekend. "I saw all the pink bats and wristbands on Mother's Day."

"I bought one last year," a middle-aged woman said.

Alex turned her way, a polite look firmly in place. "I didn't know they sold them."

She nodded. "The money goes straight to research to find the cure. You lost your wife to breast cancer, didn't you, Lieutenant?"

For the life of her, Lisa had no idea how the woman knew this. Her stomach clenched in sympathy for Alex, but she'd lived in a small town all her life. There was no such thing as a secret in Jamison, New York.

"Her name was Jenny." His face said the rest, the look of pained memory setting his jaw, his gaze. "She was beautiful. And kind. And she loved us more than life itself. I hated saying goodbye."

His simple, heartfelt words misted the room. Eleven women gazed up, seeing his loss in the set of his shoulders, his sorrowed expression, each one wondering how their battle would end. He stepped back, raised a hand to prevent Lisa from following him and moved toward the entry. "I'll call you. I didn't realize you were tied up and this can wait a few hours. Nothing major."

His short speech alluded to the theft, but Lisa read the meaning behind the words. He'd walked in on a big part of her life tonight, her campaign to fight an insidious disease. The look on his face said he'd fought his battle and lost. And no one could blame the man for not wanting to fight again.

He left amid a flurry of goodbyes, words that changed to appreciation once he was out the door.

"Talk about gorgeous."

"And then some."

Lisa had to smile because, yes…Alex was easy on the eyes.

"And ripped," added Sabrina. "Yum factor of off-the-charts on a one-to-ten scale."

"Oh, he's that all right." Viola grinned as she handed out a cup of tea. "He mows the lawn in his

T-shirt on his day off. Twila claims she turns the fan on extra high."

"And what do you do when Alex mows his lawn?" Lisa wondered out loud.

"Pretend to garden." Viola winked as she proffered the last cup. "With my glasses on, of course."

"Oh, of course." Lisa laughed outwardly, but inside? Deep inside she was wishing this stupid disease away, wishing she was whole again, wishing...

Sabrina interrupted Lisa's inner turmoil as she reached for her tea. "My daughter Lana is in Becky's class. They're in the same reading group and she says Becky talks about her mother all the time. But in the present tense, as if she was alive. She said the teacher explained it to them one day when Becky was out sick, that Becky must miss her mother a great deal to pretend like that."

Lisa's heart squeezed tight at the thought of Becky's charade. Why would she pretend? Why would she hide the loss of her mother?

Kids hated to be different. Lisa knew that. They longed to blend, be part of the crowd. What kid wanted to be looked at? Talked about? Especially when you were the new kid in class?

The reluctance fit Becky's personality, her inner neediness to belong, to be special. How sad that she might think otherwise over circumstances beyond her control?

"That's how I knew about his wife." Jeannie Sedgewick swept the group a knowing look. "My daughter runs the pre-school just outside Wellsville. His little boy stays late, trying to introduce Alex to all the single moms. My daughter says the little guy checks out who's married, looking for the next Mrs. Steele."

The next Mrs. Steele.

Jeannie's words snapped Lisa back into reality. Alex's aversion to breast cancer was understandable. He needed clean and fresh, unsullied by the travesty of disease. Maybe life didn't come with guarantees, but there was nothing wrong with starting anew. Better for him. Better for her. A clean slate.

"So…" She put a smile in place, an act she'd perfected during her illness and Evan's abandonment. "How shall we set this up, ladies? Organized or loose?"

"I vote organized," Amy said. She raised her hand high. "And I've got a suggestion. How about if we kick off our announcement of this group with a breast cancer awareness float in the Fourth of July parade next month? If we borrow a farm wagon from Lisa—"

"Consider it done."

"And I'll call the parade director and see if they'll approve a late entry," Viola added. "Can't see why they wouldn't but we all know that the committee likes its i's dotted and its t's crossed."

Their quick acceptance of Amy's idea deepened her smile. "We can decorate it the weekend before the Fourth, and that will make us the face of breast cancer in the Southern Tier."

"Putting a face to something makes it harder to ignore," another woman pointed out.

"She's right. I'm in." Jeannie raised her hand halfway up. "And I'm off for the summer in two weeks, so I'll be glad to shop for the balloons, streamers, ribbons, etcetera."

"Awesome."

A chorus of agreement rounded the room.

Amy indicated the notepad on Lisa's lap and lofted her electronic tablet with an overdone sigh. "I'm taking notes tonight, Lisa. With a click of a button I'll send them all to your emails. Put that throwback-to-the-eighties paper stuff away."

Lisa tossed the notebook onto the floor and raised her hands in surrender. "Never let it be said I want to hog all the work. So… What shall we call ourselves? We'll want banners to display on the float, so we need an official name. I was thinking the Southern Tier Breast Cancer Corps. What do you guys think of that?"

Her question instigated a flurry of comments, effectively moving the attention to the basics of meeting protocol and goals. The conversation helped keep her on track while her heart pushed aside the look she'd seen on Alex's face. He'd been startled, yes. Surprised by the circle of women. The look in his eyes said he abhorred this disease for good reason, but it was a look Lisa knew too well. And one she never wanted to face again.

He'd handled that poorly, Alex realized as he drove into town. And for a cop, there was no excuse. He should have worn his game face when he walked in that room, but the last thing he expected was a room full of breast cancer patients staring up at him.

Remembering, his chest tightened. But he shook the old feeling off, knowing he'd blown it. Lisa couldn't help the disease any more than Jenny could. Or the rest of those women. And she was willing to launch an all-out attack by raising money and awareness, teaching a community by setting a good example.

What had he done as a result of Jenny's hard-fought battle? He'd run, fast and hard, hoping to leave the vestiges of cancer behind. Yet here it was, meeting him face-to-face in a war of wills. He had no intention of allowing an intangible to best him. Which meant he better suck it up and deal with things as they came along.

He pulled into a parking space outside the General Store, a quaint shopping experience in Jamison. He strode into the historic mercantile, greeted the owner with a brisk nod and moved straight to the candy jars. "John, may I have a half pound of those, those and those?"

"Sure, Lieutenant." The store owner opened a brown paper bag, old-school style. "In separate bags?"

"All in one is fine," Alex assured him. He grasped the bag, paid the bill and turned to leave, but John stopped him by clearing his throat. Alex turned back.

John waved a hand westward. "Any luck with the theft of the Fitzgeralds' equipment?"

Alex shook his head. "Not as yet. You got any ideas?"

"None." John hesitated, then shrugged. "We've been talking, though, about what we might do to help." His glance swept the town outside his door. "Except no one's got cash to replace expensive stuff like that."

"And they most likely wouldn't like charity," Alex added.

"But making a claim is as good as asking to be dropped from some insurers these days," John went on. He walked Alex toward the door. "It's tough when you own a small business. You become a liability real quick and that's no good in today's market."

Alex had thought Ozzie's assessment on making a claim was overdone, but seeing the same expression in John Dennehy's gaze told him otherwise. "We're following leads, but they've been thin."

"Well, we'll get the word out that folks need to

think harder. Someone had to see something. The Fitzgeralds do a lot for this town."

Alex couldn't disagree, but he understood the limits of deep-sleep, pre-dawn hours. Whoever took Lisa's equipment did so in the dead of night. Not too much got noticed then, unfortunately, but this glimpse into small-town protectiveness heartened him. He wanted that for his family, a new beginning in a place that looked after its own, where kids climbed trees and sold lemonade on the sidewalk.

He turned the car around, headed west, parked and strode up the Fitzgeralds' front walk and rang the bell a second time that night, but this time he didn't wait for someone to answer the door. No, this time he walked in as if he belonged there and he knew exactly what conclusion the gathered ladies would draw from that maneuver.

And he refused to care.

They turned his way as he aimed for the centered coffee table. He opened the paper bag and poured a pound-and-a-half of breast-cancer-awareness-wrapped candies onto the table. "I figured if Lisa could support two causes at once—" he smiled and hooked a thumb her way "—so could I. When it comes to fighting cancer, folks have to stick together. Right?"

"Right!" Viola fist-pumped the air, grinning.

"I like how you think, Lieutenant." The middle-aged woman who'd asked about Jenny reached over, grasped a candy bar and held it aloft. "This isn't on my diet, but I'll rob from tomorrow's points."

"You do what you've got to do in this life." Alex flashed her a grin, then turned Lisa's way.

He'd shell-shocked her. He knew it, and liked the feeling. Getting to know her, he was pretty sure not too many men could keep pace with Lisa Fitzgerald comfortably.

He could.

He moved her way, pushed a lock of hair behind her cheek and held her gaze for long, pointed seconds. "I'll call you later. Okay?"

"Of course." She blushed, clearly unaccustomed to this kind of attention in front of a group of people. Which only made the situation more fun. Should he kiss her and put the ladies over the top?

No, he decided. He was pretty sure these women figured out why a guy would ride to the candy store and drive back, just to add to their table of treats.

And it wasn't simply to support the cure. It was to support a vibrant, beautiful woman who seemed to be capturing more of his heart every day.

He turned, gave the ladies a little salute that made them sigh out loud and smiled. "Ladies. Good night."

"Good night, Alex."

"Thank you!"

"God bless you, Lieutenant."

He turned at that last and exchanged a soft smile with the middle-aged woman. "Right back at you."

As the door shut behind him, twelve pairs of eyes focused on Lisa, because Caro had come in from the kitchen, and all twelve women were looking for answers.

Well...

"Isn't he just the hottest thing since Chinese mustard?" she asked out loud.

A chorus of laughter and agreement mixed in reply, and Lisa knew the outcome of Alex's bold move. Speculation would abound by tomorrow. In small-town U.S.A., everyone knew everything at rapid-fire pace.

Chagrin vied with joy inside her. He'd staked a claim of interest tonight, publicly. But hearing how Becky and Josh were handling their new situations was a wake-up call. They were pretending resilience, much like she saw in Emma. *And in yourself,* her conscience scolded.

True enough.

But kids' needs should always come first. And if Alex was unaware of Becky's pretense and Josh's reasoning, someone should set him straight.

A sheet of pink floral paper fluttered to the floor as Alex grabbed laundry from the girls' room late the next morning. Emma's childish script covered the paper, front and back. He reached out to set the note on her desk, but his actions were hard-stopped by two little words: *Dear Mom...*

His heart paused. His hand wavered. The words

blurred and he wasn't sure if it was his shaking hand or moist eyes that caused the words to go indistinct, but it didn't matter. He sank to the edge of Emma's bed, let the laundry slide to the floor and read the letter.

I'm starting to get used to the school here. Kind of. Mr. Henery isn't like Miss Dougall, but he's nice. He doesn't know about a lot of the books I like to read, but he knows a lot about science and he lets us do experiments in the creek. I think that's my favorite thing so far.

I made a friend, too. Her name is Sophie. Her mom died when she was little and she came to our house to help us plant gardens. The other kids look at me weird because I don't have a mom, but not Sophie. She likes me with or without a mom.

Alex's heart constricted and he had to read that simple sentence one more time. "She likes me with or without a mom." Was it really like that for Emma? Were kids that cruel or clueless?

Sometimes. And he should have thought of that before now. Why was he so much better at hearing criminals than his own children?

Becky is still a brat. She makes Josh cry on purpose. We planted a garden around the house and I'm taking a class soon, all about grow-

ing stuff. Becky's coming, too, even though I didn't want her to. Dad said she could. I don't know why.

Do you miss us? Is heaven nice? I think it is. I miss our puppy so much. I bet she misses us, too. Especially on Saturdays.

I'm sending you hugs and butterfly kisses, just like you used to do to me. When you were alive.
Love,
Your daughter,
Emma

Alex had no idea how long he sat there, holding the paper, eyes wet. His thoughts jumbled, pondering her words.

She was writing to her mother. Her deceased mother. Was that normal? Good? Bad? He had no idea.

The poignant prose revealed things she'd never said out loud. Like the teacher. And still adjusting to the changes he'd instigated.

Reality speared him. Emma was giving him her game face, much like he did on a regular basis. Her pretense that everything was all right covered the reality of a ten-year-old with a lot to handle.

By your choice.

Guilt mounted as he stared at the letter. He'd given away their dog. He'd picked up and moved them away from everything familiar, not realizing the possible emotional consequences of the action. In his grown-up head, starting fresh and new made sense. Grief had worn him to a nub, and the dark side of his city assignment wore on him. He'd been drowning, plain and simple, in a pool of darkness. How foolish of him not to understand that children thrived on continuity, that removing them from everyone and everything they held dear might sucker punch them.

And dear, sweet Emma couldn't talk to him about it, so she wrote unseen letters to her late mother.

He stood and paced the room, mentally sorting options, but there were none at this point. He couldn't exactly pick up the family and move them back to Fairport again. His job in Troop E had been filled, he had a responsibility here and he'd made promises he needed to keep. And he'd bought a big, old, rambling house. No, he had transplanted them fully.

But there had to be a way to make this easier.

He set the letter back on the floor, peeking from the edge of the bed skirt where he'd found it, tossed the laundry into a white wicker basket and carted it to the first-floor laundry room.

"Let not your hearts be troubled..."

The simple words of St. John's Gospel pinched Alex's soul. How could he be so blind? Was he truly a man who refused to see what was right before him? His children's anxiety? Their inner thoughts and dreams? Was he so blinded by his desires that he negated their stress and emotions?

Yes.

The admission saddened him. He could do better. Would do better. These children were his heart now, God-given gifts linking him to Jenny. How could he have minimized the effect his choices had on them? More than anything else, he should be uplifting them. Helping them. Protecting them at all costs. Not the other way around. And here he was, thrusting them into a new home, new schools, new church, new friends—

And he'd kissed Lisa, knowing he shouldn't rush into anything because he'd already transplanted his kids into a shaky new normal.

He threw a load of laundry into the machine, started it and decided he needed to implement a plan. He wasn't sure what or how, but clearly it needed to be done. The sooner the better. And for the moment, that plan couldn't include his growing feelings for Lisa.

Chapter Nine

Lisa couldn't ignore the early morning abdominal ache that gripped her, but that's precisely what she wanted to do. Pretend away the soreness, swallow a pain reliever and will the discomfort away.

And then hope it wouldn't come back. Ever. Except she'd felt it repeatedly the past few weeks.

Cancer treatments could mess things up. She knew that. Hormones got jumbled and body enzymes were bumped and jostled to thwart a recurrence.

The centered pelvic pain pushed her mentally back to the warning of uterine cancer, a caution the pharmacist reprinted each time she filled the prescription for her ongoing chemo drug. She'd shrugged it off then. She didn't dare shrug it off now.

"Are you okay?" Ozzie walked into the kitchen as Lisa downed two ibuprofen with a glass of sweet tea a few minutes later. "Headache?"

"Yes." The falsehood made her cringe inside. Her head felt fine, but if she told him she'd been experiencing repetitive pain for no good reason, he'd worry. And that was the last thing her grieving father needed to do with everything he had on his plate.

Besides, she recognized the foolishness of being overly concerned. A few cramps were nothing to get riled about. Except when one shoe fell on a cancer diagnosis, patients waited for the other shoe to drop. But it couldn't be anything serious. Not now, when she was facing her five-year mark?

Cancer doesn't read calendars, it is what it is. But wouldn't it make more sense to find out for sure and stop worrying? You're being absurd. You know that, right?

Lisa hushed the voice that sounded like one of her mother's common-sense edicts. She'd wait a few more days, see if the pain increased. Right now, the ache was dull. Slightly above a three on the one-to-ten scale, constant enough to instigate a fear she'd tabled nearly three years ago. What if the cancer had spread?

She pushed the worry aside, kissed her father's cheek and pocketed her cell phone. "I've got the grocery list here—call me if you think of anything else, okay?"

"Will do." He moved toward the garden store while Lisa aimed for her SUV. Determination marked each step. She'd navigated that first year post-cancer, where every little thing seemed like an imminent threat. Weird moles? She had them removed. Twinges? She'd pause, wondering if they were a sign. Headaches? She'd spent a few weeks sure the disease had moved to her brain only to find out she had a mild sinus infection exacerbated by mental stress.

She'd put the brakes on in year two, shoved off concern and readjusted her attitude, but this pelvic tension stirred up those early anxieties. The warning on her chemo had advised a multi-year window for the uterine involvement. Back then she'd decided to fight one beast at a time. The off-chance of a later problem dimmed in the harsh light of a current spreading cancer.

But the thought of facing life-threatening illness again dismayed her. She needed to wrap her head around that on a personal level before sharing her fears. She'd give it a few days. If the discomfort abated, she'd forget about it. If not, she'd call the doctor. Everything had been fine at her last checkup, and her sensibilities scoffed at the idea of a new cancer spot. But she knew the travesty of dealing with treatments once, and recoiled at the thought of a repeat performance. So she'd give herself a little time, and swallow painkillers to calm the reminder that something was amiss internally.

She called Alex's home early the following week, determined to keep things simple while she finished her project with his delightful daughter. Emma answered on the second ring.

"Emma, it's Lisa."

"Lisa!" Childish enthusiasm pitched her voice higher. "Are you coming over today?"

No. Not until she gained a better grasp on her emotions around Alex and his family. Maybe her physical discomfort was God's way of warning her off, nudging her away from those sweet children. If so, mission accomplished. "I'd love to, but I've got Rosie tonight. I'm afraid we won't accomplish much with a toddler around."

"Tell me about it." Emma's voice adopted a big-sister tone. "Between Becky and Josh, I can't get a thing done. They're so pesky."

Lisa laughed. "Well, they're younger. It's kind of how that goes. I needed to ask you about that little front garden, the crescent-shaped one that's visible from the road. We should plant it soon, and I don't have anything indicating what you wanted to do. Did we miss it?"

Long seconds ticked by. "I, umm…have a plan for it."

"Yes?"

Another space of time made Lisa arch a brow. "Kid, I'm getting older as we speak. Out with it. It *is* legal, right?"

Emma laughed, but Lisa heard the reluctance in her voice. "Can I email you the ideas?"

Whoa. Lisa might not be a mother, but she'd been

a kid and she knew a slide-by when she saw one. "Is your father right there?"

"Uh-huh."

"And you want to run this by me privately?"

"Yes." The single word gushed out on a breath of relief. "Then if you don't like it, we'll do something else."

"Send it over." Lisa headed for the office area as she spoke. "If I have questions or concerns, I'll call you back."

"Okay." Her voice faltered again, but not as long. "I'll send it soon."

Nearly an hour had passed by the time Lisa made it into her office. She pulled up her email, saw Emma's name and clicked to download and print the girl's ideas. As the picture rolled out of the wireless printer, Lisa realized why Emma had held back.

She'd created a pink garden to honor her mother. Staring at the blotches of shaded rose, Lisa saw beyond the gesture of respect. She glimpsed the heart of a motherless child, a girl who'd been wrenched from everything she knew and loved and brought to a new place. Emma's loss was palpable in the comma-shaped garden, where mauve and rose "wave" petunias were backdropped by taller pink flowers.

Emma missed her mother.

Lisa missed her mother, too. Her life had been so busy since Christmas, trying to do all and be all so her father could grieve, that Lisa hadn't taken time to fall apart.

She did that now, at her desk, with Emma's garden print catching her tears, wishing little girls could always have their mamas. And big girls, too, because saying goodbye to your mother always came too soon.

She understood Emma's calm, press-forward attitude because it mirrored Lisa's. But should a kid have to be stoic?

At thirty-three, maybe.

At ten?

No way.

Determined to whack sense into Alex Steele's thick head, she called him. He answered on the first ring. "Lisa. Hey. I've been meaning to get in touch with you."

Meaning to get in touch meant he'd been putting it off, but she refused to let that bother her. Right now, this was all about Emma. "Can I see you to discuss something?"

"The case?"

"No. I figured if there was an update on the equipment, you'd have called me or Dad. About Emma."

"Sure." He sounded relieved. His relief painted a sharp picture for Lisa. He didn't want to revisit the kiss, no matter how nice it was. And it had gone way beyond nice, on her end anyway.

Nor did he want to move forward from there,

because he'd have called. Why did that insult her when she'd made a personal decision to back away from this attraction on her own?

"How soon can we meet?" She tried to keep her voice detached while every muscle in her body wanted to thrash common sense into Alex's head.

"I'm free for an hour at twelve-thirty."

"I'll meet you at Connealy Park, just below the shaky bridge."

"You're coming unarmed, right?"

He was being funny, but she had a reason for wanting an open venue. They both worked in busy places with lots of ears. She didn't want anyone to overhear what she had to say to Alex. Between Emma's reticence, Becky's imaginary mother and Josh's willingness to hunt for a new mother among the preschool moms, someone needed to put the children's needs first. That someone was their father.

And he'd most likely hate her for saying so, which only made this day worse.

She wanted to talk, but didn't sound too friendly.

Well, why would she? He'd seesawed over this relationship for weeks, drawing close, then backing off. Why wouldn't she throw her hands in the air and be done with him?

She probably had. So had he. But something kept drawing them together, tempting them. If only—

"Here's a lead on your girlfriend's case." A slim

folder smacked down on Alex's desk. "I expect you'll find her equipment parked behind a small rental house a mile east of Kirkwood Lake."

Iuppa didn't try to veil his dislike. Therefore Alex did. "What makes you say that, Sal?"

"This guy answered an online ad for farm equipment. He thinks the farmer is over in Erie. Even offered to deliver a gently used T190 for a reasonable price."

"You placed an ad?" Alex stood and gave credit where due. "That's excellent. I didn't think of that."

The admission made him vulnerable in the detective's eyes. Alex knew it would. But honesty and hard work had gotten him here. He wasn't about to change that now, regardless of how much the investigator resented him.

"I know these towns, Lieutenant." Iuppa faced Alex. "This is my territory. I was born here and I'll most likely die here. If you need to know something, you go to the people who know the towns." He slapped his chest. The gesture took Alex back to the Tarzan movies his father loved and his mother hated. "Me. And the others like me."

Alex lifted the folder. He opened it and scanned the contents. "Why would this guy steal from the Fitzgeralds?"

"Why does anyone steal?" Iuppa looked surprised by the question. "Money. Cash. Maybe he's a druggie. Maybe he's just a guy down on his luck and behind on his mortgage. In any case, he's got the exact piece of equipment we're looking for. I say we go get him now and ask questions later. Before he has a chance to get away."

Alex shook his head. "Check him out first. If he's our guy, we'll nab him, but the T190 isn't rare and I don't want to collar someone for a coincidental posting online. See if you can find a reason why he'd do this. How he'd know when to come on-site and trailer that stuff out of there. It was a bold move."

"So bold no one saw a thing," Iuppa griped. "Sneaking around at 4:00 a.m. isn't bold. It's cowardly."

Alex shrugged. "Not when you're driving a rig big enough to haul away farm equipment on someone else's land." He raised the folder slightly. "Do you want to follow up or shall I do it?"

"Give it here." Iuppa grasped the file and raised his voice just enough to draw attention their way. "Might as well. I've done the legwork so far, haven't I?"

Alex refused to look around. He knew what he'd see. Some of the guys were okay with him coming in from outside. Others weren't, but that wasn't anything new or different in cop circles. He needed to earn trust and respect. Having Sal dress him down while trying to show him up in front of others?

Classic underling envy. Iuppa had strategized his move when the office was fairly full of people, hoping to embarrass Alex.

Not gonna happen. If Iuppa put together solid facts to lead to Lisa's equipment, Alex and Jack Samson would be grateful. But he wished he'd thought of putting an ad on the internet himself now that a space of time had passed.

He pulled into the parking lot to the left of the suspension walking bridge about an hour later. He spotted Lisa right off.

Beautiful. Tall. Regal.

She carried herself more like a queen than a princess, and he loved that about her.

Right until she saw him and frowned. No, make that glowered. She marched his way and thrust a paper toward him, then snatched it back before he could make out the image. Her first question took him aback. "Do you have any idea what your kids are doing, Alex?"

Beautiful? Regal? Shrew-like might be more accurate at the moment. She waved the paper again. "Any clue at all?"

"Stop yelling and tell me what this is about." If she refused to stay calm, he had to. At least long enough to figure out what was wrong. And then he'd walk away and leave well enough alone because she clearly was less enamored of him than he was of her, which was exactly what he wanted, wasn't it?

Until her lower lip quivered with hurt and indignation and then he just wanted to pull her into his arms and comfort her. For hours.

"Here." She pushed the paper at him again, and this time let him take it. He turned it around, studied the design and shrugged.

"What is this?"

She sniffed, disgruntled, as if the answer should be obvious. "A garden."

He acknowledged that with a slow nod. "I see that. And?" He lifted his gaze to hers, puzzled. "This makes you angry?"

"You make me angry."

She sputtered the declaration as if *he* was the one with issues. He studied the garden plan, then the woman in front of him before lifting his shoulders. "I don't get it."

"Exactly!" She nodded, emphatic. "That's the problem, Alex. You don't get it, but you're doing absolutely nothing about it, and that's unacceptable."

"Stop railing at me. Please." He kept his voice calm, a trick-of-the-trade in police work, but inside, anger simmered low on a back burner. Who was she to scold him? Berate him? He'd held it together when Iuppa one-upped him a little while ago, and when the guy sought to embarrass him at Miss Mavis's place, sending out a full contingent to save Alex from a blind woman's empty gun. But he must have missed the calendar update that declared open season on Alex Steele in Allegany County. "There's no reason we can't keep things civil between us, is there?"

"Civil? Us? What are you talking about?" Her

outrage blended with bewilderment, then she took a step back. Way back. She waved a hand between them. "You think this is about us? You and me? There is no 'us,' Alex, despite a kiss that rocked the scales into the stratosphere. This is about them." She pointed to the paper again. "Your children. And how their lives are completely messed up."

Her accusation flashed the simmering anger to boiling point. Alex's practiced cool and calm snapped. "What do you know about my kids? About any kids? You're not a mother, Lisa."

"I know this." She stepped closer, and ticked off her fingers, holding his gaze. "Josh asks the single moms at pre-school if they want to date his daddy because he needs a mommy like the other kids and he wants to help his daddy find one."

"He's four," Alex sputtered. "He doesn't understand what's happened and he just wants to be like the other kids. He'll grow out of it. Or find me a date. Either way, problem solved, right?"

His attempt at humor failed miserably. Lisa's expression hardened more, and he hadn't thought that possible.

"Is it funny that Becky pretends her mother is alive? That she wants the kids at school to think her mother's home, waiting for her at the end of the day? That she tells stories about her mother, present day? As if Jenny's the one taking her for haircuts, buying her clothes?"

Alex's anger withered. The thought of Becky

lying to save face, pretending Jenny was alive...
"How do you know this?"

Lisa met his gaze, raised her chin and sighed. "I
think you're the only one who doesn't know this,
Alex. The kids in her class are treating her with
kid gloves because the teacher explained how she'd
gone through a difficult loss, but Becky doesn't
know that. In her head, she thinks they believe her
because they're playing along."

"Why didn't her teacher tell me?" Alex strode
off a few paces, whipped around and raked a hand
through his hair. "How dare she address a problem
like this without talking to me first."

Lisa shrugged. "Maybe she was hoping it would
pass. Maybe you're not so easy to talk to. I have
no idea. But two of the ladies at Tuesday night's
meeting were aware of the situation. And if they're
aware, that means most of the town knows."

"That my kid is making up stories? Inventing a
mother that doesn't exist? Great." Alex's attempt to
wrap his brain around her revelations failed. "Why
would everyone know and not say anything?"

"Because they like you."

His short, bitter laugh doubted her assertion.
After dealing with Sal's tirade at the barracks, he
was pretty sure few people in Jamison liked him.
"Right."

"They do." Lisa hauled in a deep breath and indicated the town with a nod. "They respect your work
ethic, your rank, the fact that you're trying to start

fresh with your kids and that you handle them well. So they're staying out of the way. Trust me—" she gave a half sigh and a small smile "—it isn't always low-key gossip in a small town. They're actually cutting you some slack. But then there's this." She indicated the paper with a glance. "Emma."

"Emma did this?"

"With my computer software originally. Then she cut and pasted pics off the internet to make the garden plan. It's a pink garden, Alex."

He stared at her, then the paper, then her again. "For Jenny."

"Yes." Lisa bit her lip and turned slightly, staring at nothing, then drew her gaze back to his. And what he saw there wasn't empathy—it was pain spiced with a dash of anger. "She was afraid to bring it to you, because it would hurt you. We've got a ten-year-old kid who can't approach her father about doing a tribute to her deceased mother because she's protecting you. And you know what, Alex?"

He was doing triple time trying to make sense of all she was dumping on him, but she wasn't done. Not by half, because she moved closer and locked gazes with him. "I'm so tired of people not wanting to deal with cancer. Of the looks…the fear…the questions people are afraid to ask outright, but wonder about behind closed doors. These kids should be able to come to you with anything. Talk to you. Share with you. But you're so busy starting new, you've forgotten to respect what's gone on before. And your kids need you to do that. They need to be able to talk about their mother. Remember her. Share those good times."

"They've always been able to talk to me." Alex made the declaration outright, but the proof was here. Right here. Lisa was holding up a mirror and the image he saw in that glass wasn't the happy family he'd been striving for. And worse?

He couldn't prove her wrong because he'd found that letter two days before. A letter written by a little girl, addressed to her late mother.

He sank onto the park bench and breathed in and out. "How do I fix this? If you're done yelling at me, that is."

"I'm not yelling. Well. Not anymore, at least." Lisa drew the words out. "But someone had to lay it out for you. If the teachers weren't willing to tackle it, and the kids were holding back to protect you, someone needed to open your eyes to what was going on. I hate that it was me, but hey. That's what friends are for, right?"

"Friends." He tipped his gaze up, then glanced down, indicating the seat beside him. "Well, friend, have you got any advice for me? Words of wisdom?"

"Talk to them."

She didn't take the seat and he understood the silent message behind her reticence. He had issues he needed to resolve. She had no desire to be thrust into the middle of them, and rightly so. And this fit with his decision to quietly back off what could have been a growing relationship, because kids shouldn't have to go through cancer repeatedly.

"Emma wants to do a pink memory garden, a breast cancer awareness garden." Lisa swept the paper in his hand a quick look. "In the front yard. That's going to be a topic of conversation when folks see it. And she'll want to talk about it. About her mother. You need to be ready for that."

Lisa's words reminded him of what Nancy had said before he'd moved the whole family two hours southwest. That he could run from the past, but he couldn't hide.

He'd been insulted then.

Now he realized he owed her an apology.

He'd been determined to wipe the slate clean for a forward thrust, but had no idea how it would affect the children's grieving. That they would think the topic of their mother was off-limits because he wanted to start new.

A grown-up might have understood his logic. How foolish of him to think kids would grasp that reasoning naturally. On top of that, he'd given their puppy away. That made him a colossal loser.

He stood and held the garden outline aloft. "Thank you for bringing this to my attention."

She bit back a sigh and shrugged. "You're welcome. Kind of. I hated to do it, but when I got Emma's email I realized I'm doing the same thing with my dad. Treading softly so he can have time to grieve for my mother."

"And you, Lisa?" Alex cut the distance between them by moving forward when what she needed him to do was step back. Stay back. "Have you had time to grieve?"

She hadn't, but as an adult, she could reason things out. "I'm realizing I need to deal with similar issues myself. And if it's tough for a grown-up, how much more difficult must it be for a kid?"

"I'll fix it." Alex didn't step closer, but she wished he would. And wished he wouldn't. He folded the paper in half and slipped it into his pocket. "Will you take care of putting together the stuff for the pink garden?"

"Yes."

"Thank you."

"You're welcome." She started to move off, toward her car. He called her name.

She paused, wanting to turn back. But she didn't. Not with so much on her plate. So much on his. She'd been alive for over three decades, long enough to know life doesn't always follow a fairy-tale path.

She needed to walk away from Alex, set him free to embrace the future God planned for him. A future that didn't include another cancer patient. A future that couldn't include her.

Chapter Ten

Alex called a family meeting that night. He'd spent every quiet minute of the day wondering how to approach the kids. Now that the time had come, his gut rumbled. His hands grew sweaty. He sat them down in the family room, then drew up a chair, facing them. "I need to talk to you guys."

Two nervous faces looked back at him. Josh, nonchalant and totally not getting it, reached for his game system. Alex got his attention when he put the small console out of reach. "Not now, bud."

Josh scowled.

Becky twitched.

Emma hummed.

His window of time was rapidly closing and he had no clue how to handle this. Him, a cop, a trained, experienced investigator. He could go one-on-one with a felon and emerge triumphant. Talking to his kids about their insecurities?

That was hard. "We need to talk about Mommy."

His words got Emma's attention. She sat up straighter and met his gaze. "I miss her."

So far, so good. He nodded. "Me, too. And I moved us down here so—"

"We could forget her," Becky supplied helpfully, her toes curling around the rungs of the stool she'd perched on. "Start new."

"No, I—"

"And find a new mommy, maybe." Josh offered his own take on the situation.

"No, Josh, it's—"

"We don't need someone new, Josh!" Becky glared at him from her higher vantage point. Alex heard the anger in her voice but her look held fear. Fear of being found out, of having kids discover her mother wasn't waiting at home for her at the end of the day.

"Emma, Lisa came to see me today."

Emma froze in her chair. She attempted indifference but he read the "uh-oh" look in her eyes.

"She brought me the sketch for your garden. The pink garden."

She looked trapped. Caught. And Alex hated that a ten-year-old kid hadn't felt secure enough to come to him herself. "I love it," he continued with a smile of approval. "What a great tribute to your mother, Emma. I'd like to get it planted this weekend, okay?"

She hauled in a breath, surprised, then nodded. Her face brightened. "Yeah, that would be great!"

"And Becky, will you help us plant stuff? Pink stuff?"

"Like at Lisa's store?"

"Exactly like that." He remembered how the pink immersion made him recoil a few weeks ago. He'd been acting like a wuss. Now it was time to man up. Lead his children, his family. "And, Beck, you know that people will see the garden, right? From the road and the sidewalk?"

She nodded and shrugged. "Yeah. It's in the front yard, Dad." She rolled her eyes like he was slow on the uptake, a typical Becky move.

"They'll notice it," he continued, leading her step-by-step, waiting until she made the connection. "They'll ask about the pink garden and we'll tell them we did it for Mommy and all the women who've had to deal with breast cancer. Okay?"

Realization dawned as he watched. She glanced at the paper rendering, then snapped her fingers as if a light bulb moment occurred. "How 'bout we put it in the backyard, by the creek? That would be prettier, don't you think?"

She cast him a bright smile, but he read the anxiety in her false cheer. The garden would call her out, would let everyone in her class know she'd been making up having a mom.

"It's going out front, Becky. That's where I planned it and that's where it's going. Besides, these are flowers that need sun." Emma shrugged off her sister's idea. "The creek is shady."

"We can change the flowers." Distraught, Becky darted a glance from the garden plan to the backyard. "Or find a sunny spot by the creek."

Emma groaned.

Alex reached over and lifted Becky from the stool. "You're worried people will find out that Mommy died, aren't you?"

Emma looked surprised. "Dad, everyone knows that. Don't they?"

Becky curled closer beneath his collar.

"And you think it will be awkward if people find out this way?"

"I don't know what you mean." She muttered the words into his shirt, but he knew she was getting his drift. In Becky-fashion, though, it needed to be her idea, in her time frame.

He'd follow her lead and go step-by-step. He held her close and aimed a firm look in Josh's direction. "And you. Stop trying to get me dates at pre-school, although I admit the brownies and cookies the ladies have sent have been a nice plus. If I want to date someone, I'll just do it, although I appreciate your help, bud."

"Like Lisa." Brows hiked, Emma arched a bright smile his way, and her eyes said the idea of having Lisa around worked for her. It worked for him, too, but kids didn't see the whole picture.

He and Lisa did. Where cancer was concerned,

once was enough. Except when he was around Lisa, he forgot that. And it had been five years since her treatments.

If you're looking for guarantees, buy tires, his conscience scolded. *There's no warranty on life. It is what it is.*

But chancing more tragedy for his children couldn't make the short list.

By the time he got the kids into bed, he was drained physically and mentally, but he'd acted on Lisa's advice and that felt good.

His phone rang. Iuppa's number flashed in the display. Alex bit back a groan. It had been a long day already, but his job didn't allow him latitude to ignore the call from the in-your-face detective. "Sal. What's up?"

"Just wanted you to know that the guy who answered the ad for the Bobcat used to work at Gardens & Greens."

A connection. At last.

"Yes." Iuppa sounded smug, as if he hadn't been instructed to research the guy more thoroughly. "He worked there for over five years, then started his own landscaping business on the side."

"Competing with them?"

"Yes. He fished from their customer base, trying to lure their customers away. Mrs. Fitzgerald threatened him with a lawsuit for infringement. He backed off, but his business failed two years later."

"So we've got a revenge motive and lack of money."

"And he'd know that Mrs. Fitzgerald died," Iuppa continued. "She was involved in all kinds of things and the local paper did a nice write-up on her. He'd know they were short-handed."

"Perfect timing." Alex blew out a breath. "Good job. You want to make the arrest?"

"Will do."

Iuppa sounded calmer. Happier. Alex hoped that was the case. And he'd make sure that their superiors knew who broke this case. True, it wasn't exactly capital murder. In small-town rural areas, this was a more likely crime. But Alex had put in years facing the murder and racketeering gig in Rochester. He was okay with the lighter staff and diminished crime in the Southern Tier.

"They've made an arrest in our stolen equipment case," Ozzie told Lisa the next day.

"And the equipment?" She knew better than to hope it was local and intact. No one took pricey equipment like that to use. Farmers had too much respect for one another. No, whoever stole their Bobcat and mower had cold, hard cash in mind.

"Seized for evidence." Ozzie's voice pitched up in relief. "Alex is hoping to get it released to us sooner rather than later."

"It's not sold? Or broken down for parts?"

"That's how they found it, actually," her father explained. "Sal Iuppa put an ad online for a gently used Bobcat. This guy contacted him through a phony email and they traced it."

"They tempted him out of hiding," Lisa mused. "I'm amazed. I figured it was long gone and we'd have to make a claim in the next couple of weeks. Who took it, Dad?"

"Greg Miller."

The familiar name had Lisa making a face of disbelief. "You're kidding. He worked here for years."

Her father shrugged both shoulders. "He was always mad that your mother let him go. That she was successful and he wasn't."

"You and Mom made this place successful with your work ethic, your fair prices and your selection of product." Lisa moved to his side and slung an arm around her father. "Teamwork built this business, Dad."

"It did." His gaze took in the sales tables, loaded with new planting ideas, fresh items for summer gardens and fall veggies. "But I'd be dishonest to pretend I don't worry about keeping things going without your mother. Making Adam work extra isn't the answer. He has a career. A family. Another baby on the way. And you and I can't handle this alone."

"We're not alone, we have lots of help and we'll hire another manager if necessary." Lisa met his look of concern frankly. "We've got Rosie and that new baby to think of. They might not want a family business in twenty-some years, but if we let it fall apart, they won't have the chance to decide that. And I," she looped her arms around him in a hug, "have loved this business since I was old enough to help out, so we'll do what we have to do. Just like Mom would expect, right?"

"Right."

She hadn't fully convinced him, but he sounded more assured. And his jaw looked stronger. Firmer.

May had been crazy busy. June sales promised an even higher rate of return. From now until Christmas, their lives revolved around the region's growing and harvesting schedule. And once the holidays were done, they planned how to make the next year just as strong.

Recovering the equipment would be a huge relief, one less thing to worry about, but Lisa understood her father's anxiety. They were in month two of a banner year, and long months of little rest stretched before her. No way could she be sick, or laid up by disease. Anything more than a cold couldn't be allowed to happen. Not this year.

"Are you all set back here?" Caro poked her head into the preliminary planting barn the first Monday in June. "I've got twelve kids lined up, ready and waiting."

Lisa waved a hand from the far end of the potting room. "Bring 'em on."

Caro slid open the barn door. A chorus of young voices exclaimed as the kids rushed in.

"Dirt!"

"Rocks!"

"Lisa!"

Emma charged forward. She looked wonderful, Lisa decided. Happy. Content. She grabbed Lisa around the waist, hugged her, and then stepped back, hands dancing in the air. "Lisa, the pink garden is so pretty! And Dad used black mulch on the dirt so the pink really stands out. I think it's the prettiest garden of all!"

"Good." Lisa smiled a greeting to the lone boy in a sea of eight-to-twelve-year-old girls, then spotted Becky heading her way. "Becky. How's it going?"

"I don't have to work with my sister, do I?"

Lisa aimed a slight frown down. "Hi, Lisa," she deadpanned. "How are you? Wow, this looks like fun. And would it be okay if I work on my own today?"

Becky raised one shoulder. "Yeah. That. What you said. So will it be okay if I work alone?"

"You've all got your own stations," Lisa announced loud enough for the whole group to hear. "Look for your names and I need you to tie back your hair if necessary and put on the gloves and aprons you'll find at your place."

"I'm over here." Emma moved to a garden bench in the back row next to Sophie Calhoun.

"And I'm up here!" Becky sent her sister a sassy look from the front row.

"With the other little kids," Emma drawled. She

put on her gloves with a "why me?" look aimed at Sophie. "Please tell me Rachel isn't like that."

"Worse." Sophie tugged on her gloves with a similar dour expression. "Eight-year-olds think they know everything."

"Unlike ten-year-olds," Lisa whispered, ducking her head between Sophie and Emma. "Who really *do* know everything but are calm, cool and collected enough that they avoid teasing younger kids in public forums."

Emma and Sophie grinned. "Okay, we'll stop. Promise."

"Thank you." Lisa moved to the front, started the project and was amazed when the first parents arrived at six o'clock. "Oops. Time flew. Two minute cleanup," she called out.

The group scrambled to put their current project either on a marked shelf or on their table to take home. For two minutes, pandemonium reigned, but when the timer buzzed completion, the gardening shed was back in order. Mostly.

"How did you do that?"

Alex's voice, his breath, his scent, near her left cheek. She could turn right then and be close. So close. Instead she took two steps forward before turning. "We practiced cleanup drills. I lose track of time and parents need to be able to drive in, grab their kids and go. After today we'll have drive-through pickup service. That way no one has to get out of the car."

"So if I want a chance to talk to you, I'd better do it today?" Alex asked.

Lisa waved a hand at the wall clock as she hugged kids goodbye. "Talk fast. I've got to gather supplies for a session I'm doing tomorrow at the adult-care facility just outside of Wellsville."

"You help there, too?"

"Not as often as I'd like." She rolled up her plans and stacked them alongside the big easel at the front of the room.

Alex noted the easel with an arched brow as the girls headed their way. "Old school. No Power-Point?"

"Not with dirt and kids." Lisa laughed as Becky pretended to be insulted. "I have the layouts done for each project and I blow them up and print them for the easel. The kids have a scaled-down version at their station."

"You enjoy this."

Lisa turned as she leveraged the sliding door closed behind them. "I love this," she corrected him. "Getting dirty, working with kids, teaching about plant life, eco-systems, worms and slugs…"

"I didn't even croak when I picked up a slug, Dad," Becky cut in. Her face showed delight as she gazed up at her father. "And the worms felt like wet spaghetti. I didn't groan like Emma and Sophie did."

Emma refused to engage the back-and-forth. Instead, she turned toward her father. "Dad, this was great. We learned about decomposers, how worms and bugs eat flesh and vegetable matter to make top soil."

"Yum."

"Dad, it *was* really awesome." Becky reached up and grabbed his hand. "And we told Lisa how pretty the pink garden is. That you got black stuff so the flowers would be more noticeable from the road."

Lisa aimed a gaze of approval at Alex. "Well done."

He wanted her approval.

He realized that tenfold, standing there. This woman had battled a killer disease. She could have easily put it all behind her. Most people would have.

Instead, she took it upon herself to continue the fight. Wage war on cancer. She'd lost part of her body, suffered indignities of treatment and was dumped by a husband who didn't appreciate her.

And she'd just given him a look that said she was proud of him, and her expression of approval pleased him.

"Dad, what's for supper?"

"Grandma made chicken and biscuits."

"I hate them." Becky sighed, dramatic. "Can I have PB and J instead?"

"I love chicken and biscuits." Emma raised her voice in appreciation. "I'll eat yours and mine, because that will make Grandma feel good for helping."

"Whatever, Emma." Becky did her characteristic eye-roll as she climbed into the backseat of the car. "You're such a Goody Two-Shoes."

"And on that note…" Lisa stepped back, waved goodbye to the girls and started for the front parking lot. "Have a good night."

He hated watching her stride off. Hated having to leave her at all. Hated…

"Dad, what are we waiting for?"

What was he waiting for? Everything to be perfect? Ideal? Absolute? That didn't happen in real life. Real life was, well…real.

He pulled the car up front, shushed the girls and followed Lisa into her office.

She turned, surprised.

So he surprised her a little more by wrapping his arms around her. Kissing her. Losing himself in the kiss he'd been longing to repeat for weeks.

Too long. It had been way too long since he held her in his arms, tucked against his heart. His soul. When she tried to pull back he whispered her name against her cheek, her ear, one hand cradling her head, while the other wrapped around her waist.

The whispered plea worked. She relaxed in his arms and returned the kiss fully. And when he finally loosened his hold and stepped back, he locked gazes with her. "Why did we wait so long to do that again? Because I've been dying for a repeat."

"Because we shouldn't have done it the first time?" She posed that as a question, holding his gaze but not holding back. "Because you've got a family to care for and I've got health issues you can't handle?"

He started to object and she lifted a hand up to quiet him. "Correction. Health issues you shouldn't *have* to handle again and that your children shouldn't concern themselves with. Bad enough they dealt with illness and loss once. As grown-ups, we can't put them in the position of facing that possibility again."

"What if common sense is wrong?" Alex said with candor. "What if we're meant to be together but we're both Type A competitive perfectionists who think they can control the world so we second-guess our destiny?"

"Put that way…" She smiled and stepped back more fully. "Alex, if it was only us it would be different. You know that. But it's not. And I don't kiss people casually."

"There was nothing casual about that kiss. Not on my end, anyway."

"You know what I mean." She reached a hand up to his face, his jaw. "You tempt me, Alex. You tempt me to imagine what life *could* be like but then I think of those kids and all the adjustments they've had." She lifted her shoulders. "And that puts up a big red stop sign."

"Luckily, signs are removable." He caressed her cheek one last time, letting his hand linger along her jaw. A tiny muscle in her throat twitched with his touch and he had to resist the urge to kiss her again. Kissing Lisa could become a habit he never wanted to break, but she was right to bring up the kids. He'd never done anything at turtle pace, but on this she was correct. Full speed ahead could mess up the tentative inroads he'd made with the kids' healing.

Taking things slow would be the better way. Right now he hated the truth in that, but hadn't he been praying for guidance?

Yes.

Then he needed to heed her plea for time. And patience. And he had two weeks of picking the kids up every day. Time to wear her down?

Yes.

He moved to the door, smiling. "See you tomorrow. And we should be able to have the equipment released from the evidence barn once the techs have completed their reports."

"That would take a big strain off around here. Thank you, Alex."

"You're welcome."

He left, glad he'd followed his instincts. Cornered her in her office. Stolen a sweet kiss that made their commonsense edicts seem most un-sensible. When he got back to the car, the girls were quarreling. Again.

Surprise, surprise.

He took out two boxes of Reese's Pieces and tossed them into the backseat. "Supper's late because your brother has soccer so stop fighting, eat these, and tell me about worms and slugs and all the cool stuff you learned. I bet you can't wait to go back tomorrow."

"I can't." Emma's voice held a surety he appreciated. "I love learning about this stuff. Becky's the one complaining."

"About?" He tried to meet Becky's eye in the rearview mirror, but she'd slouched into her seat, her face mutinous. "Uh-oh. What happened while I was inside?"

"Ask her." Emma jerked her head in her sister's direction. "I sat in here reading. She got out and went to look for you."

"You did?" Alex paused the car at the parking lot edge. "Becky, didn't I tell you to stay in the car?"

"Yes." She met his gaze in the mirror and her little face looked pinched and miserable. "And I saw you, Dad. I saw you kissing Lisa."

"Say what?" Emma turned his way. "Dad, were you really? Way to go!"

"I—"

"Don't pretend you weren't." Becky sat straighter in her seat, ready to challenge him. "It was disgusting."

"It was kind of nice, actually," he corrected her, keeping his voice matter-of-fact. "And I do believe you're the one who keeps telling me I should get a life. Right?"

"I didn't tell you to kiss someone." She pretended a self-strangulation, her little hands gripping her throat, totally over-the-top Becky. "Eeuuww. I thought you only wanted to kiss Mommy."

"I did." Oh, man. How did a grown-up explain this to a child? That one love doesn't stop when another love begins? Because he realized in that office, while kissing Lisa, that he loved her. Wanted her. Needed her. And now he'd gone and messed up his kids. Again. "It's complicated, Becky."

"It's not," she insisted. "When I grow up I want to fall in love with someone who will love me forever. Just me. And if I die I want them to still love me."

Emma sighed. "Here we go. It's always all about you, Becky. How about for once it's about Dad?"

Becky harrumphed, clasped her arms around her chest and burrowed into her seat, chin thrust out. When he pulled in the driveway, she burst out of the car, stormed up the walk, pushed through the door and ran up the steps. The slam of her bedroom door ricocheted throughout the house.

"You're home." Nancy met him at the door. She slanted a look upstairs, angled him a look of empathy and waved to the kitchen. "Let me take Josh to practice. You guys eat. I gave him a sandwich after school, and it will be snack time by the time he's done with soccer. Is that all right with you, Alex?"

Alex accepted her gracious offer, relieved. "It's perfect. I'll give that one—" he swept the upstairs hall a quick look "—time to settle down. And I know Emma and I are starved."

"Good."

Josh raced down the stairs, a size 4 soccer ball clutched in his hands. Alex paused him long enough to realign his socks over the shin guards and hug him. "Have fun, bud."

"I will!" He raced to the back porch, a bundle of preschool energy.

"Actually, I'm not all that hungry, Dad."

Alex turned, surprised. He met Emma's gaze and read the confusion there. She wanted him to move on. Be happy. The two-year age difference between her and Becky allowed a different perspective. But even so, change would be hard.

Turtle. Turtle. Turtle.

He nodded and kept his expression easy. "You relax. It's been a long day for everyone. The nice thing about chicken and biscuits is that they're just as good reheated. If you decide you're hungry in a little bit, we'll eat then."

"Okay." She grabbed him around the waist, and held tight in a hug that said so much. "I love you, Dad."

He knew that. Felt it. But it was nice to hear the words. "I love you, too, honey."

The sound of Nancy's wheels on the asphalt drive meant he had ninety minutes to contemplate how he'd messed everything up. Again. But looking back, would he have chosen differently? Decided not to follow Lisa into that office and kiss her?

Not on your life.

* * *

That kiss.

Amazing. Wonderful. Marvelous. Delightful. Strength blended with gentleness and warmth, the combination of senses that made Alex Steele special.

And unavailable.

She'd called the doctor's office that morning. They'd ordered a few tests and set up an appointment for the following week. She'd prayed all day, hoping her cancer hadn't spread, and that the drugs hadn't compromised her uterine lining.

She needed to keep her distance from Alex. How wrong would it be to invite his attention, knowing she might have a problem? And the girls would be at the Garden Center for two long weeks, right up until the day of her appointment. The drive-through pickup should help. She could have Caro or one of the employees keep an eye on the pickup time, make sure it went smoothly. Staying out of sight might keep her off Alex's radar.

Alex had just finished folding a load of towels when Nancy pulled in with Josh. Josh spotted Becky on the backyard lawn swing. He raced for her, chattering a mile-a-minute, extolling his feats of strength at Super Tot Soccer.

Alex went outside to save the kid's life. Becky's face and stature said she didn't want to entertain tales of his prowess and before she had time to deflate his growing four-year-old ego, Alex steered him toward the house. "Ice cream sandwiches in the freezer, bud. Toss your soccer stuff in the laundry room and grab one, okay? But don't eat it in the family room."

"Great!"

Josh raced for the back door. The kid moved nonstop from dawn until dusk, and rarely at a walking pace, a bundle of high energy. His limitless vigor made him perfect for a soccer field. Alex turned Becky's way as Nancy approached from the driveway. "Are you ready to eat?"

"I don't want food." She hauled her legs up into a folded position and clamped her hands around them, fingers knit, face drawn. "I don't want stupid chicken and biscuits, I don't care about ugly, slimy slugs and worms, and I want you to stop kissing Lisa."

Silence rang.

Nancy went still beside him. Very still. He stood there, caught for a moment, wondering which course of action to take. Kill the kid or soothe the mother-in-law's shock?

The kid, he decided. But he wouldn't kill her. Prison didn't go easy on lawmen. Instead he sank down onto the swing beside her and bundled her up, protesting, into his arms.

He didn't say a thing. Not one thing, because this wasn't about explanations. It was about time and loss, change and adjustment. A part of him wished

Becky hadn't left the car and witnessed the kiss he'd shared with Lisa.

Another part understood that change would be hard on her no matter when or how it happened. Why not now? He cuddled her and set the wide swing rocking, to and fro.

Nancy said nothing. He met her gaze and hoped Becky's words hadn't hurt her too much, but he recognized the pain in her eyes.

Jenny's eyes, a generation removed. Eyes that had been passed down to two of his children.

She didn't say a word. She didn't look mad—she looked...hurt. Resigned. And sad. Oh, so sad. And her step as she walked away?

Heavy and laden, as if the weight of the world just resettled on her shoulders.

So much hurt. So much pain. So much responsibility lay at his door, weighting his life. His choices. But he wouldn't lament why things couldn't be simple. Not now. Now he'd simply cradle his little girl and let her cry.

Chapter Eleven

Nancy pulled into the nearly empty parking lot of Gardens & Greens and sat there, staring at the varied displays, unsure why she'd come.

She noted the signs of breast cancer awareness. The plethora of pink ribbons. The vendors' pledge to contribute to the fight-for-a-cure campaign.

Too little, too late for her beautiful Jenny, worn down by a regimen of treatments that made fighting the disease scary, distasteful and painful. To lose that fight had been the ultimate kick in the head. Not so much to Jenny, at least at the end. Jenny rose to the occasion like she always did. Nancy? Not so much.

She'd been mad at God. Soul-riddled angry. Confused. Battle-worn. And now, just when she noted the first signs of healing between her and Alex, he was falling for another woman. A replacement for her daughter.

Reason told her that was normal.

Loss pierced her, because mothers don't get replacements. There were no second chances. Jenny had been her one and only, born before science could do miraculous things to help mothers have children. She'd been given one child, one beautiful girl-turned-woman, then lost her too soon.

Her heart rose up, choking her. She didn't know what she was doing here. Did she want to see Lisa? Talk to her? Yell at her?

"Can I help you?"

She turned. A man stood outside her door. His face showed concern. He leaned down. His glance left indicated the garden store. "We just closed, but it's light for another hour. If you want to look around, you're more than welcome. I was just going to water the annuals that haven't sold yet."

"You don't mind?"

He shook his head and opened the car door for her. "Why should I? No sense wasting daylight, now is there?"

She shook her head as she climbed out and choked back the rise of angst in her chest. "No. That would be silly."

"Ozzie Fitzgerald."

Lisa's father.

He put out a hand. Nancy accepted the gesture and raised her chin. "Nancy Armstrong."

"Well, Nancy, I'm not sure what kind of project you're working on, but we should have something that fits." He strolled down the brick path, waving left and right. "Lisa's got perennials over there." He turned slightly. "The shrub-and-tree lot is on that side, and we've got major plantings out back."

"Major plantings?" She tipped her gaze up to his and realized he had a gentle brow. A strong chin. Late-day shadow marked his face, a brindled mix of gray and brown, but what was left of his hair still held the brown. And he didn't do a comb-over across the front, in an awkward attempt to hide his bald spot. The hair surrounding it was classic flat-top, military cut. And it looked really good on him.

"The big trees and bushes we use for landscaping contracts. Pricey."

"Ah." She understood pricey. She'd been blessed with money all her life. Funny how it meant so little now. Her husband gone, her daughter deceased. "I expect they're beautiful."

He smiled and didn't disagree, but she saw something else in that smile. Something lost and a little worn. "My wife had a knack for all this." He paused his steps and his gaze wandered the beautiful grounds and displays surrounding them. "Now Lisa does the planning. I do the grunt work. But yes, the things my wife did?" He turned back to her and shrugged. "They're beautiful."

"She's gone."

He nodded, shoved his hands in his pockets and rocked back on his heels. "January. Kind of sudden. I'm not sure what to do with myself some days."

Nancy understood that dilemma too well. "I

know. People tell you to pick up the pieces and move on, but where are those pieces, exactly? And move on to what?"

He met her gaze with one so gentle that she wanted to cry and smile all at once. "Why to tomorrow, of course. Whatever God's got planned for us. Are you planting a garden, Nancy?"

She nodded. Gardens were the last thing on her mind when she pulled into this parking lot, but standing here, chatting with this man, she'd talk about anything to elongate the moment. "I'm thinking of it for when I get my new place. Is it too late?"

He shook his head. "It's never too late. You just adjust the plant size and hike up the watering schedule. Planting a garden is like raising kids. You just have to work a little harder through the dry times. Have you got a family?"

Did she? Yes and no. "Grandchildren. Three of them. They, umm…" *Say it, Nancy. Spit it out. Face the truth.* "My daughter died of breast cancer two years ago. So it's just me, my son-in-law and the three kids."

"I'm sorry." He turned her way completely, and his face said he understood the pain she couldn't mention, but his next words surprised and saddened her. "Our Lisa had breast cancer. So far she's been lucky, but I pray every day that it doesn't come back, that she has a chance to live her life. God's promise, right?"

She shook her head, not understanding.

"Life to the full," Ozzie explained in a commonsense voice. He leaned down and clipped off a fading hydrangea blossom, then removed a picture-perfect one and handed it to Nancy. "When my wife got sick, she stayed strong. Tough. A fighter. But when it was Lisa that was sick, Maggie cried every night. Never in front of Lisa, though. She was so mad, so outraged that she couldn't help Lisa more. Mothers hate to see their children suffer, and Maggie was no exception. She attacked that disease with Lisa, probably just the same as you did with your daughter."

Nancy nodded. She'd done all she could, and still failed. But she was here to talk about it, and this nice man's wife had died. "Yes."

Ozzie gazed westward toward the sinking sun. "When I try to reason all this out, I come up blank."

"Me, too."

"But then I see all this." He waved a hand to the beauty of mixed floral tones. "I see our little granddaughter, Rosie." He raised his shoulders again. "And I realize I may never understand things in human terms, so I have to accept that God numbers our days. Not me. Not doctors. Not treatments. And that makes it easier although I've never been one to hand over controls easily. Except with my wife, and I learned early on that it was better not to get in her way."

His words made perfect sense to Nancy. And

peace surrounded him, despite his loss and his daughter's struggles.

Warmth stole into her, a seeping goodness of possibilities. She'd been so angered by what she lost, she'd forgotten to celebrate what she had. Her health. Her grandchildren. Her finances, a commodity she'd taken for granted for decades.

Ozzie thrust his chin toward the greenhouses. "Nancy, would you like to help me water?"

"I would. Yes." She jumped at the offer and smiled up at him. "That would be so much fun."

He grinned. His chest pumped up as he hauled in a breath, and he scraped a finger and thumb to his chin in a sweet gesture, pure country. "Well, don't let it be said I don't know how to show a lady a good time."

She laughed.

So did he.

A last piece of her heart burst free, opening wide, welcoming the late-day coolness and the bird chatter fading to frog-song. And then she went to water flowers in her gray silk paisley top and white capris and didn't care if she water-stained them. Not when she was helping Ozzie take care of what was his.

Chapter Twelve

Lisa's cell phone jangled shortly after six the next morning. She tossed the toothbrush down and grabbed the phone, certain there must be an emergency.

"Hello?"

"Top of the mornin' to ya, Lisa!" Alex's voice came through loud and clear as he pseudo-rapped a line from a popular Christian song she had on her iPod.

She burst out laughing and sank onto the edge of her unmade bed. "How did you know I love that song? And that I'd be awake?"

"Farm girls wake up early," he told her. "And the song came from Emma. She says you walk around humming it all the time."

Did she? The obvious answer was yes. "It uplifts me."

"It's great and I just added it to my computer. Hey, about last evening…"

"When we shouldn't have kissed?" she mused.

"I was actually calling to schedule another round because we waited far too long between the first and the second. I do believe we agreed on that."

"We agreed to no such thing," she returned lightly despite the discomfort she was feeling yet again. Hadn't she just taken two pain relievers? "I can't factually disagree with your logic, but that might be lack of coffee talking."

She heard the smile in his voice. "Go get your coffee. Greet the day."

"And Alex?"

"Yes?"

She faltered, then added, "I wanted to thank you and the guys for finding our equipment. Having it back will mean a lot to us."

"Wasn't me, but I'll pass the thanks on. Bless you, Lisa."

His gentle blessing made her falter.

She wanted that very thing, to be blessed with the health so many took for granted. To not have to think and question every stupid symptom or sign. Right now she felt trapped, ensnared, longing to move forward but caught in the unknown.

You're scared.

She hated to admit that, despising her fear. Fear equated weakness.

Or maybe it's normal, her conscience suggested. *Maybe it's okay to be afraid, but grab onto faith. Isn't everyone afraid now and again? And maybe*

*it's time to stop pretending a strength you don't
have and let God help.*

She gripped the phone tighter, wishing. But the
need for regular pain relief reminded her she had
no right to move further with these feelings. Not
now. Probably not ever. "Thank you, Alex. Back
at ya. And hey, it was nice seeing Nancy here last
night. She was pulling out as I pulled in."

"Nancy was there?" His voice changed. Deepened. "You're sure?"

"Positive. Not too many cars like hers around
here. She was most likely scouting out plant and
flower ideas. Dad doesn't mind if folks browse
when we're closed. And she told me last week she
was house-shopping."

"She is." His tone suggested there was more to
the story.

"Well, there you go."

"Yes. I'll see you later when I pick the girls up,
okay?"

He wouldn't because she'd make sure he didn't.
Not because she wanted to, but because she needed
to. No one with a heart and soul could justify running that young family through cancer's wringer
intentionally, but she said goodbye lightly as if everything was fine.

It wasn't.

Nancy had gone to see Lisa.

Mixed emotions formed a perfect storm in Alex's

gut. Hadn't he just congratulated himself on better relations with Jenny's mother? They'd found neutral territory, the beginnings of mutual peace, and now this.

"Dad! I can't find my brown boots and I need them for science today. We're going in the creek!" Emma yelled the question down the stairs because coming and finding him and speaking in a normal tone of voice didn't enter into her getting-ready-for-school mode.

"What's for breakfast?" Josh raced into the kitchen clutching a tattered stuffed bear from his toddler days. He scrambled onto a stool and eyed Alex, expectant. "We like French Toast Sticks. A lot."

"Got 'em." Alex reached into the freezer as Becky rounded the corner. She slumped into a chair, a well-practiced look of utter dejection wrinkling her features.

"Do I have to go to Lisa's class today?"

"You signed up. You go. End of discussion."

She pouted, but dropped the subject and he wasn't sure if that was good or bad. Would she corner Lisa today? Make a scene there?

Bad enough that Nancy had gone there to confront Lisa. He tamped down a rise of negative emotion, reminding himself what Nancy had lost. And his mother-in-law was making a life-changing commitment to move closer to them, to be part of her grandchildren's lives. For that reason alone he needed to keep their relationship uplifting, but how could he if she insisted on interfering? And what would she have said to Lisa if they'd come face-to-face last night?

That thought made him shudder inside. He'd talk with Nancy today, before he picked up the girls from their gardening class. Better to get things out in the open than let them smolder.

He stopped by Nancy's apartment in Wellsville later that day and rang the bell.

No answer.

He scanned the parking lot for her car.

No car.

He picked up Josh, avoided two single moms that Josh kept insisting he meet and aimed the car toward the Fitzgeralds' garden store. He'd been waiting for this moment all day, anticipating the time when he could see Lisa again.

He smiled, hopped out of the car in the parking lot, then grabbed Josh before the four-year-old made a mad dash across the pavement. "Hey. This way."

"But Grandma's here!"

Alex turned. Stopped. Stared.

Nancy's car was parked across the lot. Unless someone else drove a boat-length steel-gray brand-new luxury vehicle, and there weren't too many of those chasing around the roads of the Southern Tier. The breast cancer pink ribbon logo in the back window confirmed it: Nancy was here. Right now.

Thoughts of a peaceful resolution fled Alex's

brain. Why had she come? To confront Lisa? She knew what time class ended. Was she here to challenge both of them in front of the kids?

He grabbed Josh's hand and strode toward the back barn. This was it. The end. The final straw. No way was he willing to let Nancy's meddling make things worse with Lisa. As if Lisa hadn't been through enough already. As if—

A familiar laugh rang out behind him.

Alex turned, puzzled.

Josh broke free and raced left. "Grandma! Hi! You're here, too!"

"Joshua." She paused a conversation with another woman, scooped Josh up and held the boy lightly as if she hadn't a care in the world.

Alex moved her way, amazed at her audacity. Hadn't she understood his directives? How could he make things clearer? He needed a chance to raise his children his way. Without undue criticism from her or anyone else.

"Well, this is a beautiful boy," the second woman noted, grinning at Josh in Nancy's arms. She switched her gaze back to Nancy and indicated the flowers in her cart. "And you were explaining about the hostas."

"Yes." Nancy nodded, emphatic. "Shade or part shade for the best look. Full sun and a hot summer are tough on hostas."

"They're tough on me, too." The other woman

laughed. "I'm going to go check out what kinds Lisa has back there."

"A bunch," Nancy promised. "Check out the Patriot series. I bet you'll love them."

"Thank you."

Nancy turned Alex's way, her face bright. Animated. Happy. Alex couldn't remember the last time he saw Nancy relaxed and happy, and because he was expecting a very different expression, he paused, confused.

"Alex! You're here to pick up the girls. You know where they are, right?"

Of course he did, but he was still trying to wrap his brain around finding her here, grinning. And wearing a Gardens & Greens smock. "I—"

"And who is this handsome fella?" Alex shifted the direction of his gaze as Ozzie crossed the busy front sales area. "Howdy, partner. I'm Ozzie."

"I'm Josh." Josh stuck out a hand. "And this is my dad. He's Alex."

"We've met." Ozzie aimed a broad smile in Alex's direction. "Your daddy's been a big help to us."

"You needed a policeman?" Josh's brows arched high. "Were there bad guys here?"

Ozzie shrugged off the little guy's concern with a half truth. "We lost something. Your daddy and his friends helped find it. Alex." He turned and put out a hand. "Good to see you, but I can't have the help being bothered by family during working hours." He sent a teasing look to Nancy and she blushed.

Blushed.

Before Alex could wrap his head around that, Ozzie went on, "Nance, would you like to grab a bite with me later? We'll never get out of here before closing and I did promise you food in exchange for labor."

She bobbed her head, clearly delighted by the prospect. "That's fine, Ozzie. That will give me time to deadhead the greenhouses and help with the watering."

"You're working here."

Nancy turned. So did Ozzie.

Alex swept the two of them a look of disbelief. "You really are? Working here?"

Nancy hugged Josh, then set him down. "Ozzie and I got to talking yesterday, and he offered me a job. The minute I started today, I wondered why I hadn't done this sooner." She aimed a smile straight up at Ozzie. "I love working with plants. Getting dirty."

"God's perfect timing." Ozzie returned her grin before shifting his gaze back to Alex. "You know it's drive-through pickup today, don't you? Lisa tries to make it easy for parents with crazy schedules."

"My guess is that Alex is in no hurry," Nancy offered, but the way she said the words, like it was all right that Alex wasn't rushing in and out, made him turn her way again.

She met his gaze. A soft smile said she understood what he hadn't had a chance to say. That it was all right to move on, to let his heart take a chance again. That she wouldn't stand in his way.

He'd been ready to challenge her, go toe-to-toe with his former mother-in-law, certain she was interfering again.

She wasn't and that shamed him.

The row of cars started moving as children were released from the potting shed barn. He reached over, gave his mother-in-law a hug that surprised both of them and moved toward the back of the display area. "Have fun."

She smiled at him, then at Ozzie, not caring that she had dirt on her hands and a wet splotch on her smock and that in itself was worth noting. "We will."

Alex was still trying to sort out this unexpected turn of events when he got to the back barn. The line of cars had dwindled to two, and as those kids were picked up, Caroline spotted him crossing the stone path connecting the barns to the mulch pickup area. "Here's Dad, girls."

He glanced around as the girls moved his way.

No Lisa.

Should he ask?

No. That would only get Becky riled up, but he leaned forward and scanned the inside of the barn, hoping.

Still no Lisa.

Caroline read the question in his eyes and shrugged. "I've got pickup duty this week."

"The whole week?" He said no more, but saw the confirmation in her eyes.

"Yes."

Lisa was avoiding him. Was he wrong to want to see her? Care for her? Fall in love with her?

Caroline's face showed sympathy for his dilemma, but he read something else there, too. She'd protect her sister-in-law at all costs, and Alex understood that. But a clever man didn't back off from a challenge, and if Lisa Fitzgerald needed a reason to drop those barriers, he was man enough to give her one. Starting tonight, once he got the kids settled, he had every intention of strategizing "Team Lisa." He may have never been a soldier, but a man should never miss a chance to plan a winning campaign. "Let's go, guys."

"Hey, did you guys know Grandma's here?" Josh wondered as they moved toward the front lot.

"To get us?" Becky frowned up at Alex. "But Dad's getting us."

"She's working here," Alex told them as they neared the car. "Grandma loves gardening. Getting dirty. You must get that from her," he told Emma.

The thought brightened her soft gray eyes. "I bet I do, Dad. When did Grandma start working here?"

"Today."

"Oh, that's so nice." Emma's look of approval swept the garden store. "She likes to keep busy."

Of course she did. Another thing Alex had messed up on, not thinking of Nancy's needs. How long and tedious had her days been, with no husband, no daughter, estranged from her grandchildren, and her home sold?

He'd been a jerk, but no more. Never again. From this point forward he'd weigh everything from all angles. He'd still mess up, but maybe not as often.

Chapter Thirteen

"Miss Fitzgerald?"

Lisa turned and faced the middle-aged woman behind her the next afternoon. "Yes. And you are…?"

"Sylvia Wells. I'm a freelance house cleaner and I'm your surprise home-tender this week."

"My— What?"

Her look of shock inspired the other woman's smile. "An anonymous friend thought you needed assistance and hired me to provide it. If that's all right with you, of course."

"I… Um…"

Lisa's brain circled this new circumstance.

Did they *need* help?

Yes. She'd pushed off cleaning and organizing since her mother's death. She'd done the basics weekly, but the whole place could use a good spring-cleaning. "I do need help." She frowned in the direction of the house. "But it's not exactly ready for cleaning at the moment, if you get my drift."

"I do." Sylvia dipped her chin in understanding. "I can come back tomorrow." The older woman's bright smile said it was okay to need a little time to accept the idea of a stranger in your house. "Is that better for you?"

"It is," Lisa decided. "That way I can corral the laundry and box up stacks of papers. Get them out of your way."

"But no cleaning." Sylvia looked straight at her. "That's what I'm paid to do. I don't understand women who clean the house before the cleaning service comes. Talk about a waste of money."

Lisa laughed out loud, because she'd intended to do exactly that. Sylvia's commonsense directive gave her the freedom to choose otherwise. "I promise. I'll remove the clutter and let you do your job."

"Excellent." Sylvia reached out and shook Lisa's hand. "I'll be here at 8:00 a.m."

"I'll be ready."

Lisa contemplated this gift as Sylvia walked toward the parking lot. Who would do this? And why?

The girls from the newly formed cancer group, she decided. Hadn't they had a discussion about cleaning and organizing? Letting others help?

Their combined thoughtfulness made her smile. By the time she'd finished the kids' gardening session on hitchhiker and airborne seeds and avoided Alex Steele by slipping out the back door, she had just enough energy to go from room to room, tossing things into bins. And by the time she was nearly done, the place looked much better.

Her mother had hated clutter. Maggie had been an organized, creative sort, and while no one would ever call her a clean freak, she liked to have order to the chaos surrounding her. Lisa moved into the dining room.

Her step slowed.

So did her heart.

They hadn't eaten in this room since Maggie's death. This had been her room, her pseudo-office, the quaint, vintage room holding shelves of gardening info behind handcrafted country doors. The old farmhouse didn't have a family room, so Maggie had converted an antique rolltop desk into her computer station. With the doors closed and the rolltop in place, no one would know the room underused for holiday meals had really been a vibrant office.

Everything in this room reminded Lisa of her mother. The North Country tablecloth reminiscent of short winter days and long, cold nights. The half-shuttered windows with lace curtain toppers. The soft yellow paint lightening the room and brightly stenciled flowers bordering each door frame, every window.

She'd avoided this room on purpose, because changing this room, cleaning it, meant Maggie was really gone.

Her heart broke into a million pieces standing

there. Right now she was tired of being strong, weary of being brave and drained by having so much wrenched out of her hands.

She hesitated at the room's edge. Breathed in and out. Could she do this? Should she?

"Come unto me, all who are weary, and find rest for your soul..."

Dark possibilities flooded her brain. Her doctor's office had called to confirm the ultrasound appointment for the following week. That way the doctor would have the tech's report when she met with Lisa.

Her cell phone ringtone interrupted her worries. Mandisa's lively tune filled the room, wild and free with reminders of a brand-new day, a new Jerusalem.

"Come unto me..."

She needed to trust God, rely on the perfect timing that hadn't seemed all that great lately. But was that fact or her skewed perspective?

She ignored the phone, put Mandisa's quick-step tune on Repeat and high volume on her laptop, then entered the dining room, energized.

She could do this. It was time. Past time. She made her way around the room, clearing this, storing that. When she finally found the table beneath the mess, she whisked off the winter-scene covering and replaced it with a summery floral, bright and new. She cut a vase full of flowers, arranged them and set it in the middle of the table as her father came into the house.

He paused. Then he turned, noting the lack of clutter around him. Finally his gaze rested on Lisa, and she wasn't sure if that was good or bad. Would he be hurt by what she'd done? Annoyed? Angry that she'd taken it upon herself to get things in order?

"Thank you." Sincerity deepened his simple words.

He opened his arms. Lisa stepped into his hug and felt like a corner of her world righted itself. "It's okay that I did this?"

"More than okay." He nodded. His gaze looked moist, but he raised his shoulders in a gesture of acceptance. "Your mother would have been really ticked at us for letting things go."

Lisa couldn't argue the truth in that. "I know."

"But I couldn't bring myself to do it. At first I just didn't care. Then it seemed like too much."

"Ditto. Well, someone got us a cleaning lady," she told him. "She's coming tomorrow morning, so I had to restore some sense of order to the place."

"A cleaning lady?" He frowned, then brightened. "Why didn't we think of that?"

"I did," Lisa admitted. "But I'm too stubborn to admit when I need help."

"You get that from your mother." He hugged her shoulders, opened a bright summer-plaid round tin and grabbed out two cookies. He held one out to

Lisa. "Try these. They're amazing. Nancy made them and I can't remember when I've had better."

"Supper…cookies…working together." She arched a teasing look up to her father. "Sounds like she's into you, Dad."

His smile said he wasn't quite going there yet, but Lisa read more in his look. He seemed calmer. Less troubled. And that made her feel better about things regardless of who or what caused the change.

"She's easy to talk to. Of course, she gets things because she's been through it herself." He jerked one shoulder up. "She lost her husband and her daughter, so she doesn't take life for granted. It's nice to have her around, isn't it?"

Lisa had wondered what it would be like to have another woman around, a total stranger potentially taking her mother's place. Witnessing her father's metamorphosis gave her a heads-up. No one could ever take Maggie's place. She was one of a kind. But she realized now that having someone carve a new niche in their lives, a new normal…

That seemed oddly doable.

Ozzie glanced around and frowned. "I've heard this song three times since I walked into the room. Is your thing broken?"

Lisa laughed out loud. "No. It's fine. I was just reminding myself to greet the day. Embrace change. Carpe diem stuff."

"Try the cookies," her father urged again. He held out the tin because he'd already eaten the two he'd extracted. "I'm telling you, these things help what ails you."

Lisa took a cookie and extolled on the level of excellence. Her father's smile widened as if he'd made the treats himself. When he'd gone upstairs, she picked up her phone to see who had called earlier.

Alex.

She hadn't looked purposely. The temptation to answer would have been too great.

She turned back to the dining room. It looked like it should now, a gracious room with period furnishings, country decor and a welcoming presence. Sylvia would provide the dusting, vacuuming and window-washing, all of which were needed, but clearing the clutter and the chaos from her mother's favorite corner of the house helped clean-sweep Lisa's soul.

The room looked good. Seeing that made Lisa feel better.

Step one of his "Win Lisa's Heart Campaign": hire household help because she's too stubborn to do it herself.

Done.

Step two: a pedicure from "Stillwaters," the spa just outside of Wellsville. Alex tucked the anonymous gift card into the Fitzgeralds' mailbox before he picked up the girls later that week. With Lisa's line of work, a manicure would be wasted. She'd made that clear when she showed off her Yankee-clad toes a few weeks back.

In his experience women loved pedicures and clean houses, but would rarely spend money on either. This way it was his dollar, his gift. She just didn't know that yet.

"Dad, check out these birdhouses!" Becky raced across the stone drive when she spotted him. She held a tiny tie-dyed house in her hand, the rainbow of colors offset by a shingled cedar roof. "Lisa says they're just the right size for chickadees and they don't mind having people around their nests. As long as no one touches them." She shot a look of warning to Josh.

Instantly, he set up a wail. "I didn't touch anything, Dad!"

"You will."

"I won't!"

"You better not!"

"Stop. Both of you." Alex used his tough voice, then squatted to their level. "You need to stop bickering over everything. I'm not kidding, I'm not advising, I'm not messing around. The fighting needs to stop. If it doesn't, there will be no TV and games for a week."

"A week?" Becky stared at him. She gulped. "Just for fighting once?" Despair claimed her face, as if realizing the magnitude of never picking a fight with her little brother. "Is that even possible, Dad?"

Probably not, Alex mused silently, but he had to start somewhere. "It is if you make it your goal. Stop bossing him around, and you—" he turned his gaze onto Josh "—stop pestering your big sisters and taking their stuff."

Josh's eyes rounded. He shuffled his feet. His chin dipped, then he shrugged. "I'll try."

"Me, too." Becky droned the words as if she'd just been issued a death sentence, but Alex saw the look in her eyes. She knew he meant it. Hopefully she wouldn't decide to test him any too soon.

Caroline crossed the stone path with Emma. "I love that your girls are at opposite ends of the spectrum," she declared as she held up Emma's birdhouse. "Emma went for a gingerbread house design while Becky's retro-hippie look will stand out in any garden."

Josh sidled closer to Becky. "I really like how you painted your house, Beck." He sent a sincere look of admiration to the wild-styled tiny home. "It's so cool."

The little guy's praise made Becky preen. "Wanna touch it?"

"Can I?" Delight widened Josh's eyes. "Yeah! Of course!"

"Don't break it." Becky warned as she handed it over, then stood guard, watching Josh turn the wee house this way and that.

"Birds will really live in this?" Josh turned a questioning gaze up to Caroline.

"They will," Caroline promised. "If they don't nest in it this year, I bet they do next year. With birds, you have to be patient."

"Not just with birds," Alex noted. He gave the potting barn a meaningful look. "But please pass on the word that I'm a very patient man these days."

Caro smiled. "Will do. Although there's patient and then there's too patient. If you know what I mean."

"Loud and clear." He exchanged a grin with her. "Let's just say the campaign has begun in earnest."

"Good to hear." She waved goodbye as she moved toward the house. "The house looks great, by the way."

"How did—?"

"She hasn't figured it out yet." Caro turned and paused. She kept her voice low. "She thinks her friends chipped in, but I knew right off because only a guy who's gone through the process understands how hard it is to pick up the pieces and move on. And Lisa's had a lot of pieces to pick up the last few years."

Alex recognized that. Emotional residual damage could be worse than surgical scars. "Sylvia did a good job?"

"Perfect." She winked and waved again. "You did good, Alex."

He hoped so. Where Lisa Fitzgerald was concerned, he wanted to do his best.

"They've all been picked up?" Lisa shot a smile to Caro as she entered the house, but there was no fooling her sister-in-law in matters of the heart.

"Stop being a scaredy-cat," Caro bossed her. She clucked like an old hen, making Rosie laugh out loud. "Get back in the game. What have you got to lose?"

Should she tell her?

Lisa hesitated. She clenched her hands, then shrugged, uncertain.

Caro stepped closer. "What is it? What's going on? Because don't try to pretend with me, girlfriend. I've been around too long and I know you too well. Are you okay?"

"No."

Caro's face paled. Her eyes went round. Her jaw went lax, then firmed. "Explain."

Lisa did. And it felt good to have someone to talk to, someone to confide in. She spilled her guts about the discomfort and the scheduled appointments.

Through it all Caro listened, a friend and a sister, nodding as needed. And when all was said and done, Caro zeroed in on the one thing Lisa hadn't said. "You're scared to put Alex and those kids through more illness and angst, aren't you?"

There was no denying that. "Yes."

"And afraid of dying."

Lisa's chin quivered. She stilled it, but not before Caro read her reaction. Her sister-in-law's quick look of sympathy pushed Lisa to an emotional brink she'd been denying for weeks. "Terrified, actually. Which only shows what a coward I am. And a fake. Because true believers don't fear death, right?"

"Oh, honey." Caro hugged her, and the embrace felt good. Strong. Empathetic. "You know there's a host of benign reasons that make women feel out-of-sorts."

"Yes."

"And you've made all the right moves," Caro went on. "You scheduled an appointment and they're running tests. Do you remember how often we went through this the first eighteen months after your original diagnosis?"

Lisa remembered all right. "I do."

"And those scares turned out to be…?"

"Nothing."

"Stop borrowing trouble." Caro made her point more stridently by pulling up a chair in front of Lisa, forcing her to make eye contact. "You'll have your answers soon. So you can either spend that time worrying yourself sick over what is most likely nothing, or pull yourself together, stop being a ninny and put your trust in God. Whatever happens, we handle it, step by step. Right? And since when don't you trust God's timing? His strength?"

Lisa looked anywhere but at her, then shrugged, her gaze trained beyond the window. "I'm not the same person inside, Caro. I weigh everything now. See how it measures up. I pray, but I don't really expect an answer because I'm not sure what to believe. What to trust. Every time I climb into that choir loft lately, I feel like a fraud."

Caro accepted that with a slow nod. "It's hard to say goodbye, isn't it? To a husband…a mother…"

Lisa blinked back tears.

Caro's face softened. "You are so much like your mother that it's like she's still around. Your actions, that 'get it done' attitude. But you're like her in another way, too, and that's hiding your feelings. You bottle things up, just like she did. Then they brew inside, a cauldron of emotion. But you're so busy being stoic, you don't notice."

Did she do that? Yes. "I like being strong."

Caro smiled. "You do it well. But there's such a thing as too strong. Holding too much in. When I get so riled up inside I want to punch someone, I think of the twenty-seventh Psalm."

A Psalm of trust, seeking protection. And—

"I love how the words first seek God's help," Caro continued, her voice soft. "But once he's done asking for help…"

"He asks God's shelter forever," Lisa cut in. "To live with the Lord always."

"And to wait on Him." Caro touched Lisa's arm. "Borrowing trouble is never good. You know that. But doubts happen to all of us. When they do?" She met Lisa's gaze frankly. "We need to pray more.

Cling harder. Because those doubts weigh down our days."

Lisa recognized the simple truth in her words. Carrying grief and worry alone burdened more than her heart…it wore on her soul. She'd been so busy being strong for others, she forgot to be strong for herself. Strong enough to reach out. Lean on God. How had she missed such a simple but important lesson?

Caro's commonsense profile of the situation was almost maddening, because Lisa knew she was right. "But I still need to keep Alex at bay. Until I know."

Caro huffed a sigh of impatience, a pretty loud one. Slightly aggressive, even.

"Like you said." Lisa met Caro's gaze with intent. "It's a matter of days. If everything turns out fine—"

"You'll reengage the attraction ASAP, no holds barred? Because this guy is off-the-charts wonderful. The cute kids are just total bonus."

"I will." Lisa smiled at the thought. "He is something, isn't he?"

"And then some," Caro agreed. "If you're looking to fall in love, he's a keeper."

"And if I've already fallen?" Lisa wondered out loud.

"Then Alex Steele will be a very happy man," Caro declared. "Because I don't think you're in this alone." She handed over the mail and prodded the envelope on top. "Check this out."

"A gift certificate for a spa pedicure." Lisa wiggled her toes, delighted. "From?"

Caro dipped her chin and smiled.

"Alex," Lisa said.

"I've been sworn to secrecy." Caro stood and stretched. "And all this drama makes me hungry. Except every time I eat, I wish I hadn't." She passed a hand over her still-flat abdomen.

"That's a dilemma."

"It will pass." Caro scooped up Rosie, who immediately offered protest about being separated from her toys. "Hush, you. We need to get home, feed you, change you and fall into bed. Because Mama's tired. And we've got a crazy week of packing, stowing, moving…"

"Thank you, Caro."

Caro waved off the thanks. "That's what we do, right? You and me? We take care of each other. I've got your back now." She let her gaze drop to her belly. "And you'll be at my beck and call in about six months, give or take."

"The best Christmas present ever," Lisa added.

Caro flashed a grin over her shoulder as she went through the back door. "I can't disagree with that."

Chapter Fourteen

He needed Lisa Fitzgerald, Alex decided once he'd gotten the kids off to school the following week.

She wasn't his. He knew that.

But if determination won the day, she would be.

You're willing to risk your children's well-being? his conscience berated him again. *Shouldn't they come first? Always?*

Yes, Alex decided. But putting them first shouldn't mean avoiding Lisa. Wasn't life fraught with danger? And no one knew the day or the hour of God's appointed time. He needed to think less and trust more. And wouldn't the kids benefit from having a woman around, a special woman, capable of loving them, just as they were? Lisa was that kind of woman. Rare. Invaluable.

He rerouted his morning routine and swung by Seb Walker's pastry shop, then took the scenic route to Fillmore, right by Lisa's house.

He pulled around back, grabbed the string-tied

white box and knocked lightly on the wooden screen door.

"Alex?"

Delight and surprise colored Lisa's voice. She put a quick hand to her hair, total woman, wondering how she looked at 7:40 a.m.

He opened the screen door, thinking she looked marvelous. "A gift."

She motioned him in as she accepted the box. "Anyone bearing food from Seb's pastry case is welcome here."

"Anyone?" Alex raised a brow. "So I'm not special?"

She blushed, which meant he was special.

He grinned. "I brought enough to share. Gotta go."

"You can't stay for coffee?"

He shook his head and tapped his watch. "Must work. But I wanted you to know I was thinking of you. I would have told you that over the phone, but you don't always answer my calls."

"Maybe I'm busy."

He reached out a hand to cup her cheek. Feel the softness of her skin beneath the pads of his work-worn fingers. "Then we might have to learn to grab more free time, you and me. Together."

Her smile said she'd like that, but something in her gaze whispered hesitation.

Which only meant he'd take more time. He cradled her cheek a few seconds longer, tapped her nose, grabbed a raspberry-and-cheese Danish and headed out the door. "I'll see you tonight when I pick up the girls. And don't duck out on me. You're being silly."

"You did bring me pastries."

He turned and softened his bossy order with a wide grin. "A point-earner for sure. I'll see you later?"

She faltered, then nodded. "Yes. I'll give Caro time off and come out from under my rock. Promise."

"Good. Although for a rock-dweller, you look mighty good in the morning, Lisa."

His words elicited a soft smile, kissably sweet. Once again her hand went to her hair as if wishing for a comb. "You, too."

A cell phone text from Sal Iuppa interrupted the moment. He pulled the phone out, held it up and backed out the door. "Gotta go."

Her winsome smile made him long to stay. The text said he needed to confer with Sal at Jones Memorial Hospital on a new case. He jogged to the car, backed around and hit the gas, glad he'd taken the ten-minute initiative. The sight of Lisa, surprised and pleased by his small gesture, would brighten the rest of his day.

"Who was that?" Ozzie wondered when he came in to refill his coffee cup a few minutes later.

"Alex." Lisa indicated the box on the table with a glance.

"He stopped at Seb's?" Ozzie's grin grew. "That family knows how to make a good impression," he declared. "Cookies. Danishes. And really cute kids."

Lisa couldn't disagree. And seeing Alex that morning, dashing up the steps, box in hand…

She'd felt like an Austen heroine, with her very own Mr. Darcy. Strong, rugged, proud, fierce. But while Alex could be cast as Darcy, she could never be Elizabeth Bennett. Beautiful and accomplished, waiting to catch a rich man's eye. She was a simple gardener, with dirt under her nails and a prosthetic chest.

"Oh, the newspaper called last night," Ozzie continued, a Danish in one hand and fresh coffee in the other.

"Because?"

"They're doing a story about your new breast cancer group and the Fourth of July parade."

Mixed feelings pressed in.

She'd welcome the free advertising for the nonprofit group. Newspaper involvement was a great way to reach potential members. And if the newspaper did an article, the local television stations would probably follow suit. They'd done a great job of promoting her pink-ribbon garden center campaign, so this was great news for the breast cancer coalition.

But once again she'd be in the limelight of what

Alex longed to forget. Her push for greater awareness became his Achilles' heel and she had no idea how to counter that effect. "That's great news, Dad."

He pushed through the door, nodding. "They'll call you later today. I gave them your cell number."

"Thanks."

"And we've got thunderstorms in the forecast."

"How bad?" Thunderstorms were never a welcome thing with outdoor garden displays.

Her father shrugged. "Possibly bad, but who knows? They're thunderstorms."

"All right." She grabbed a Danish and followed him, the bright morning sun making the prospect of late-day storms a non-issue. Seeing Alex, talking with him, starting the day off together... Even the darkest storm couldn't take the shine off a beginning like that.

Two kids, approximate ages three and five, found wandering the gravel road leading out of the forest preserve in the dead of night.

Alex pulled into the parking lot of the E.R., flashed his badge, and moved to stand alongside Sal Iuppa and the initial responding trooper. The sight of the small children, dirt-smudged, scraped and bruised, wrenched his heart. His protective nature jumped into overdrive. The little girl's hair, a mass of knots and tangles, made him regret every time he groaned while doing Becky's hair. The boy, small and thin, was in desperate need of a bath and a diaper change. The girl wore ill-fitting sandals. The loose faux leather had rubbed raw spots along her insteps and toes. Tiny spots of blood marked the paper drape on the E.R. bed.

The boy, barefoot, had a gash on one foot that already looked septic. Did that mean they'd been on their own for days? Or had this happened before they wandered off?

"No reports of missing children?"

Sal's low growl echoed Alex's feelings. "None."

"And they're not school age," Alex mused quietly.

"Not all folks send their kids to school, Lieutenant."

He'd encountered that in the city where drugs prevailed, but here? In Heartland, America? Alex flexed a brow, inviting Sal to continue.

"Some people homeschool their kids to keep them out of harm's way."

Alex nodded. He had friends who homeschooled their kids successfully.

"And some do it to keep their kids from spilling what goes on at home. Teachers and social workers are mandated reporters."

"Right." Alex clenched then unclenched his jaw. Raw emotion rose up inside, a force that ran roughshod over him whenever kids were endangered or maligned. "Not so different from the city streets, then." Anger snaked a path along his spine. He squared his shoulders, longing to fight on the children's behalf. He'd tended young gunshot victims on the streets of Rochester and Buffalo. Had them die in his arms, twice. He'd watched small children be placed back with neglectful parents, mothers and fathers in biology only. He thought he'd left that behind when he moved here, his heart longing for a Mayberry-type existence.

Was he foolish to think that poverty and pestilence couldn't hide in the mountains? Obviously so.

"Except—" Sal motioned him away from the small, curtained cubicle "—there's so much space out here. In the city, folks can hide in plain sight and you might never know they're there."

Alex couldn't argue because that happened all the time.

"Down here, there are miles and miles of hills. Gravel roads. Places up-mountain and tucked in woods so deep it's almost impossible to get to."

"You think they might be from a family in the hills."

"I think they've been on their own for a couple of days at least, that they're probably one of the worst cases of neglect I've seen in years, and that whatever parents they have are probably high ninety-eight percent of the time. Or gone."

"No life-threatening injuries?"

Sal shook his head. "A camper saw them. Thought it was a bear coming through the woods, then heard the little guy crying."

"Thank God."

Sal nodded, his lips thinned. "Amen. The county will be here soon to get them. In the meantime, we've got to figure out who they are."

"And meet the parents."

Sal turned more fully. "Every time I see neglect like this, I want to teach the parents a lesson personally. But then I look at the parents." He paused. Shrugged. "Usually they're so cranked crazy that I almost feel sorry for them. And I don't feel sorry for too many people, Lieutenant."

Alex didn't doubt that for a minute, but he understood Sal's reasoning. Addictions were hard to overcome. He'd witnessed that time and again in Troop E. He thought with fewer people, things would be better in the hills.

They weren't better. Just more spread out. "You tried talking to them?"

Sal grimaced. "And got nowhere. I figured a little time and TLC might soften things. The little guy doesn't seem too verbal, and the older one appears to have taken a vow of silence."

That wasn't a huge surprise to Alex. A lot of kids would do whatever seemed necessary to protect their parents from the law. He nodded, accepting Sal's decision to wait. "Shall we head back to where they were found?"

"Yes." Sal stared a few seconds longer, as if memorizing the scene. Hospital personnel, voices soft, hands gentle. The whirring click of machines droning background noise, intrinsic to health care.

The little boy's look of abject fear, eyes wide, his longish hair blocking one eye.

The girl sat straighter. Taller. The protector. Her status shone in her determined demeanor, but her eyes...

Tawny gold-brown, with long lashes and a turned-up nose beneath...

Those eyes said she geared for trouble at a moment's notice, and that stoicism, that preparedness, firmed Alex's internal decision to make their lives better. Happier. Safer. Some way, somehow.

As they approached their respective cars, Sal jerked his thumb north. "We can drop my car at the station and head over in yours. No sense taking both."

"Will do."

Alex sensed less hostility from the older detective, but was that because he was finally accepting Alex on board or because everything else paled in comparison to the two banged-up waifs they'd just left? "Will county call us to tell us where they put the kids?"

"If Fern Moriarity is on the case, she'll help us out. She's got a way with kids. Even the ones who don't dare say anything eventually spill their guts to Fern." Iuppa paused at his car and stared west, hard. "Storm coming."

"Pop-ups throughout the afternoon was all I heard," Alex countered.

"My knees took too many hits in football. They're

telling me it's something more than pop-up thunderstorms."

Alex climbed into his car and weighed Sal's warning. Was this another trick, another way to make him look stupid?

Except Sal seemed sincere.

In any case, it wouldn't hurt to warn his mother-in-law. He pulled her number up on the hands-free unit but the call went to voice mail. Would he sound foolish to leave her a message to watch out for storms when the morning loomed sunny and bright?

Maybe, but he'd rather be safe than sorry. He left a brief message, pulled into the station house parking lot, picked up Sal and headed into the hills, determined to find whoever was responsible for the condition of those two little kids.

Chapter Fifteen

Lisa got the weather alert on her phone about the same time an ominous crack of thunder grumbled from the west. Treed hills prevented her from seeing the approaching storm, but the first loud rumble was followed by a bright slash of cloud-to-cloud lightning. The ensuing rush of noise said the storm was close and moving fast.

A gust of wind barreled through trees that had been lying limp in the heat of the mid-June day. The wind came with a roar of its own. The force of it pushed the handful of mid-afternoon plant shoppers indoors.

Lisa hesitated.

Long tables of flowers stood unprotected. Displays that took hours to finesse marked every corner. They'd sandwiched most of the annuals in an allotted space between two greenhouses, but a really bad storm wouldn't be stopped by plastic-wrapped metal tubing.

"Lisa." Her father waved her in as another gust of wind brought the beginnings of rain. Clearly this storm had no plan to wander in, intensify and roll out. It hit fierce, harsh and indiscriminate. From their back window they could see the northern hills still blanketed in sunshine.

Overhead and out front?

Mother Nature raged.

Sheeting rain obliterated most of their visual. The cracks of thunder followed the lightning almost immediately, marking the storm directly overhead. It raged, nonstop, for just over twenty minutes, and when it was done, Lisa wanted to sit down and cry.

The fierce storm hadn't just toppled plants. It upended tables. Knocked over statuary. Dropped a limb from a towering black locust onto a water garden display.

The spot between the greenhouses was barely touched.

The primary entrance, loaded with flowers?

Destroyed.

The half-dozen folks gathered inside the sales barn looked dumbfounded, as if they didn't know what to do or say.

Sirens rang in the distance. That sound thumped Lisa into action. Sure, they took a blow, but these were plants, not people. Plants were replaceable.

People weren't.

And sirens meant someone was in trouble, maybe grave danger.

Her father turned. Sought her gaze. Mixed emotions marked his expression, but then a movement outside made the group turn, en masse.

A boat-length silver car cruised into the parking lot. Nancy's car was followed by Twila's. And then Gary and Susan Langley pulled in behind. Three more cars followed, and as this group gathered and headed toward the garden store, Ozzie and Lisa went out to meet them.

Eddie Jo Shupert bustled over from across the street. She was dressed in old painting clothes, rubber shoes and a big, silly hat to guard against the sun.

Except there was no sun at the moment.

Nancy reached them first. Mouth grim, she surveyed the damage as Twila, Gary and Susan flanked them from the other side. Gary glared at the mess, then jutted his chin as his gaze swept the group. "Let's do this."

Never a man of many words, Gary's expression brought a circle of nods.

"You're here to help?" A smile started at Ozzie's mouth and traveled to his eyes as more cars filed in. John Dennehy, from the village. Reverend Hannity and his wife.

"Eddie Jo sounded the phone tree alarm. Said you folks took a direct hit while most of the populated areas were spared. So here we are."

Eddie Jo.

Lisa scolded herself internally for any former

annoyances her intrusive older neighbor may have caused because right here and now, she'd saved the day. "Dad, if you can direct the guys how to reset the tables, we can load the plants onto the flatbed, bring them back to the potting shed and fix them."

"Will do."

Happy chatter filled the air as this group of unlikely garden workers hauled plants and shrubs this way and that. The women formed two lines in the potting shed, using the children's workstations. Deft and not-so-deft hands reset the plants individually. Then they wiped down any potting soil from the outside of the pot, and put the refreshed flowers back on the flatbed to make the short ride up front.

In two hours the garden center was up and running. Clean. Refreshed. And other than quickly drying puddles beneath a hot, summer sun, there was nothing to be seen of the mid-day destruction other than the broken limb Ozzie and Gary lugged into the yard.

"I don't know what to say," Lisa told the motley crew as they high-fived each other on a job well done. "I'm speechless. Thank you seems inadequate."

"Many hands make light work," Twila reminded her. "How many times have you gathered a crew to help someone, Lisa? With gardening, weeding, cancer?" She shrugged one shoulder, saucy as ever. "This time it was our turn. Sakes Almighty, I haven't been this dirty in who knows how long? Aren't we a sight?"

They were. Wet dirt marked arms, sleeves, pants and faces, but nothing that couldn't be washed off. "Eddie Jo, thank you for calling people."

The older woman brushed off Lisa's gratitude. "Glad to help."

"We all were," John Dennehy added. "When trouble hits a small town, it hits all of us. Losing your mother, then the equipment, now this…" He jutted his chin to indicate the area that had been damaged. "There wasn't much anyone could do about the first two things."

Lisa nodded, understanding.

"But this?" He smiled, and John Dennehy wasn't normally a smiling man. "This we could fix."

Lisa's heart took a wide step forward as the makeshift work crew climbed into their cars.

Three hours ago they'd suffered cataclysmic damage. Now?

All had been righted because one pesky neighbor had the good sense to start a chain of phone calls on their behalf. "Eddie Jo, thank you."

Eddie Jo brushed off the thanks as she headed home. "Like John said, some things we can't help." Eddie Jo's face said that Maggie's death and Lisa's cancer fell into that category. "Some we can. That's what neighbors do, right?"

"Yes."

"Will I see you at the kids' concert tonight?"

"Probably not."

Eddie Jo paused as if wanting to offer advice. Then she stopped herself, winked and waved.

Nancy approached from Lisa's left. "I'm going to the concert. Your dad's riding along. Would you like to go with us?" Her welcome smile made Lisa long to say yes.

Common sense held her back. Any minute now, cars would pull in with kids for the afternoon class. The timing spared her a long explanation. "I'm going to pass this time, but you have fun. The kids will do a great job."

"If you change your mind, let us know," Nancy continued. "We'll save you a seat."

Lisa read the meaning behind the words. Nancy was offering Lisa a chance to take Jenny's spot at Alex's side. The magnanimous offer humbled her, because Nancy understood breast cancer's dark side better than anyone. "Thank you, Nancy."

"You're welcome." Nancy reached out and gave Lisa's hand a quick squeeze, and that small gesture almost brought Lisa to tears, but Nancy veered off the brick path and back to the sales area while Lisa aimed for the potting shed classroom.

I will not leave you orphaned...

Holy words of promise and remembrance gathered in her heart. For a few long moments this afternoon, she was ready to throw in the towel. Toss away everything. The storm's damage had seemed too much to bear initially, as if God Himself sent them a message to stop. Put the brakes on. Do something else.

And then the convoy of help poured in, ready to make things right, and that message was clear: wait on the Lord. Trust people, trust God, trust yourself.

Her heart felt stronger, happier, more focused, all because a crew of friends and neighbors joined hands to help. Would Lisa have instigated the phone tree for herself?

Never. Her stubborn and giving nature offered help but was loath to accept it. So this was a lesson well learned. God helps those who help themselves.

She greeted the children as they arrived, feeling more in charge than she had since her mother's unexpected diagnosis. Yes, some things were out of her hands. But it was past time to revive the old Lisa, the one who not only took charge, but believed. That was the person she wanted to be.

Alex and Sal found no sign of the kids' family. No home. No cabin. Not even a tent or a makeshift trailer.

They'd gotten drenched midday, but by the end of it, slogging through trails and getting Alex's car caught in the mud not once, but twice…

He almost liked Sal Iuppa.

"You guys got caught in the storm." The captain stated the obvious as the two investigators walked into the station house midafternoon. He jerked his head left. "You've got company. Just arrived."

"Fern." Sal reached out a hand, then indicated Alex with a nod. "My boss, Alex Steele."

Sal said the words with no hint of resentment or malice, a welcome change. Alex shook her hand, waved to chairs and sat down. "What've we got, Fern?"

She grimaced. "Not much. The girl is clearly afraid to say anything and the boy is too young to say much. He appears to be nearly three years old but wasn't very verbal today."

"Understandable."

She didn't disagree. "They've been through a lot. I'm just glad someone found them before today's storm."

"Us, too." Sal hunched forward, his gaze direct. "So the girl. She's not talking? Where'd you place her?"

"With Mia."

Sal grinned. "I figured she'd be full. Glad I was wrong."

Alex raised a brow, inviting Sal to continue.

"Mia is my niece. My sister's kid. She's got a spread by Kirkwood Lake. Great place. She doesn't have any kids of her own. Her husband passed away about four years ago, and left her quietly comfortable."

"She does foster care?"

Fern picked up the thread of conversation. "Mia used to do horse therapy. A riding accident put a halt to that. Now she uses her therapy skills on broken kids, without the horses. And it works."

"When can we talk to the kids?" Alex knew they should question the children sooner rather than later, but his own experience taught him kids needed time to reacclimate. If only he'd realized that sooner…

Fern sent him a frustrated look. "Normally I'd advise waiting, but I don't think you have that option in this case, Lieutenant. I think you need to talk to them now, because who knows what state their parents are in? If they're even here at all? We've had kids dumped off before."

That reality gripped Alex. Who could do such things? Drop your kids off in the mountains and drive away? If that's what happened, were these kids left alone as attempted murder, hoping two little kids wouldn't make it out alive?

"Let's dry off and head over to the lake." Alex angled a look at the time. "I've got the girls' concert tonight. Can't miss it."

"Me, too." Fern stood and hauled a carpetbagsize purse up her arm. "It's Meaghan's last one before moving to the middle school."

"Five minutes, Fern?"

She nodded, pulled out her phone, tapped something and was talking a mile-a-minute before Sal and Alex had made it into the back room for fresh clothes. "She's not my usual experience with social workers," Alex admitted as he grabbed a new T-shirt from his locker.

Sal grinned. "She's married to a sheriff, so she understands the cop side of things. Her soft heart wants to fix everything and give those kids time, but instinct is telling her something bad might be going down and these kids might have been part of it."

"Well, they're safe now."

"And we'll keep 'em that way," Sal promised.

"Viola!" Lisa hurried forward as Viola wove between the diminishing displays of annuals late that afternoon. "What's up?"

"I wanted your opinion on this bunting for the Independence Day float." Viola held up two gathered lengths of material for Lisa's inspection. One was done in a solid pink, unbroken. The other used a range of pink strips, sewn together, a wave of pink tones.

"The stripes, definitely." Lisa's lack of indecision firmed Viola's smile. "And with the pink ribbon symbols—"

"Made with balloons," Viola added.

"Yes." That would be a feat on July Fourth, getting all those balloons blown up and attached to the ribbon-shaped frame her father had created.

"Jeannine ordered T-shirts," Viola added. "Enough for us and more to sell at festivals over the summer. And breast cancer awareness bracelets."

"Perfect." Lisa smiled, caught sight of the approaching cars and jerked her head. "Gotta go. My last session of this year's kids' gardening class."

"And you've got Alex's girls here, I see." Viola's smile broadened. "Teaching them the tricks of the trade. I saw their grandma working up front. Such a nice lady, and not afraid to get dirty. My sister said she dug right in this afternoon, helping clear away the mess left by the storm. I was down-county and didn't even realize you had trouble, it was that bright and sunny in Wellsville. That's some good people, right there."

"They are."

"You're not yourself these days, Lisa. I can see it in your eyes." Viola aimed a keen look in Lisa's direction. "I don't know what's going on, but I've known you since your mama walked you in a stroller, and these past few weeks, something's changed. Now you can either tell me or ask me to mind my own business, but maybe you've been so busy helping others that you forgot it's okay to need support yourself. Especially with Maggie gone and all."

How did Viola read between the lines? See what she worked so hard to hide? Lisa winced inside. Her eyes watered. "I'm fine, really. You know how it is. You walked the walk. Good days. Bad days. And we shrug our shoulders to both, don't we?"

The older woman stayed quiet a moment, watching her. Weighing things up. Then she pursed her lips, glanced away and motioned to acres of meadow grass surrounding the floral areas. "I can't take in all this prettiness around us and not believe in God. I see His hand in the beauty of the Earth, but I personally know the fragility of the human body. Our timelines aren't always written as we'd hope or plan. But whatever is going on…" She shifted her attention and gaze back to Lisa. "I want you to know I've been praying for you. Are you seeing a doctor?"

"Yes. Late tomorrow morning," Lisa admitted. "Dr. Alvarez."

Viola accepted the oncologist's name with equanimity. "She's ordered tests?"

"Several. I get the results when I see her." She frowned, dug her toe into the gravel and shrugged. "It's probably nothing, Vi."

"Which will give us reason to celebrate." Viola didn't make light or minimize Lisa's concern. "But in the meantime just know I'm praying for strength and blessings to rain on you like the dewfall."

Like the dewfall…

That Biblical phrase was a favorite of Lisa's. She smiled and hugged the older woman again. "I've got to get class going because there's a kid tugging my arm as we speak."

Becky Steele laughed up at them. "I can help you get started, Lisa. I'll do anything you want me to do. Okay?"

Viola smiled at the child, gripped Lisa's arm in

a show of solidarity and walked away. Lisa bent to Becky's height. "Can you do attendance for me, please?"

"Yes!" Becky strode into the shed, shoulders back, head high, as if in complete control, a wonderful step up from a few weeks back. As she checked off names, Lisa realized something else. Becky's increasing stability stemmed from her father's continued healing. Was she right to stay a step removed from the delicate balance Alex and the kids had worked so hard to establish?

For the moment, yes.

Did it hurt to quietly remove herself from a picture she longed to create? To finish?

Yes, again. But true love meant valor. Seeing Alex's kids grow in acceptance and maturity? That was a priceless gift. One she didn't dare destroy.

Alex hit Nancy's phone number on his way to interview the children. "Do you mind picking up the kids for me? Getting them cleaned up for the concert? If you're not working, that is."

"Ozzie and I are both coming, so that makes it easy." Her voice had been on perpetual upswing since starting her job at Gardens & Greens. Or maybe it was proximity to Ozzie Fitzgerald. In any case, Nancy Armstrong was happy for the first time in years. "I'm here anyway, so it would be senseless for you to drive over here unless there was *another* reason for you to drive over here…"

She left the comment open-ended. He heard the smile in her voice. The gentleness in her tone. No rebuke, no guilt.

"If I had time, I would," he confessed. It felt odd to admit that to Jenny's mother. "But we're swamped."

"Ozzie and I would like to take the whole family out for chicken nuggets after the performance. If that's all right?"

"It's so far beyond all right as to border magnificent," Alex replied. He hesitated, wondering if he should have invited Lisa. In a small town, bringing a single woman to your kids' concert was a bold statement, and while he was feeling pretty daring, the woman in question kept backing away. He had tomorrow off, but he'd planned a surprise he hoped would tip the scales toward normal with his children. Maybe they could plan something for this weekend?

He hoped so. "Then it's okay if I meet you at the school?"

"Perfect."

He hung up the phone and considered the change in her.

She sounded happy. And young, which was funny for a woman eyeing sixty years, but not so amusing when he felt old on a regular basis.

But not around Lisa. He called, later, wondering if she'd like to go to the concert with them.

No answer. Was she busy or avoiding him? Probably both, Alex mused as he entered the school with a quarter hour to spare. Courting Jenny back in college hadn't been this convoluted.

His life was different now. Looking back, he wondered if he appreciated the blessing of a wonderful woman like he should have.

No.

Knowing that, he refused to make the same mistake again. Like it or not, Lisa Fitzgerald would know she was loved and cherished, every day. If and when he got time to court her in earnest.

"Dad! Over here!" Josh's yell drew heads around. The look of excitement on his little face—

Which could go to meltdown mode in a heartbeat considering the evening hour—

His wide-open expression embraced life, love and family. Josh sprang up, hugged Alex, then climbed back on Ozzie's knee. "I can see better from here," he explained.

Alex met Ozzie's smile with a slightly raised brow. "And that's all right with you?"

"Couldn't be better." Ozzie ruffled the boy's hair and Josh squealed. "I like having kids around. Don't you, Nance?"

"Love it!" She aimed a happy look of agreement at Ozzie. "I can't remember when I've had this much fun, Oz. Being here, with the kids." She layered butterfly kisses to Josh's cheek. "And working at the farm with you. I won't know what to do with myself when the season's over."

Ozzie met her gaze and drawled his answer with pointed deliberation. "We'll spend our time getting ready for the next one, of course." He winked at her and the look of absolute pleasure on her face made Alex grin.

An empty seat yawned at his right. Josh's seat, he knew, but he pictured Lisa there, laughing, chatting with friends and neighbors, then cheering the youthful choir on throughout the show. It felt wrong not to have her there, a part of this family night. The empty seat told him he needed to take off the cruise control and leave Lisa no exit routes. He was tired of being a turtle, wearing a shell. From now on he was the rabbit, running the race with gusto.

But the rabbit lost the race, his conscience reminded him.

The rabbit might have, Alex mused as the kids took their places on the risers. But he wouldn't.

Lisa watched as Nancy, her father and Alex's girls pulled away from the garden store that evening.

She drew in a deep breath, tackled cleaning the potting barn as if her life depended on it and forced herself not to cry.

Jesus had healed the lame, the sick, the sightless. He'd cured lepers, made them well and whole.

But people died every day, in the prime of their life, like the trooper on the highway, doing his job.

Jenny Steele, a young mother, a loving wife. Lisa couldn't come close to reasoning these things out.

Her phone rang. Alex. She eyed the display and muted the phone. Most likely he was calling to see if she'd come to the concert. He didn't know how close she came to chasing the car down and begging a ride in the backseat.

But strengthening her ties to Alex and those beautiful children before this diagnosis would be wrong, wouldn't it? She pocketed the pesky phone, closed the potting shed door, mopped her eyes and squared her shoulders.

She'd know, soon. Regardless of the outcome, knowing was better than endless speculation.

Which would be fine if the concert was tomorrow night, her conscience scolded. *Are you really going to stay home and miss a wonderful community event while you wait and worry? Haven't we gotten beyond that yet? Because we should have.*

Hesitation slowed her step. Should she have moved beyond the worry stage? Did cancer patients ever get beyond that point?

Yes, she decided. They had to, or drive themselves crazy. She didn't bother changing her clothes because walking into the house might give her time to reconsider. She grabbed her keys off the hook, waved to the girl up front who was closing things up that night, pocketed her phone and drove to the elementary school. She had to park a block away, but when she walked into the old auditorium, she saw Nancy, her father, Josh and Alex seated toward the front. She wove her way through throngs of proud parents and made her way down the left-hand aisle, just in time. "Is that my seat?" She indicated the empty seat to Alex's right with a raised brow and a slight smile.

Ozzie turned, surprised.

Nancy smiled and dipped her chin.

Josh squealed. "Lisa! You came!"

Alex simply rose and waved a hand. "I was saving it for you."

Oh, those words. That look. The calm acceptance of what had been and maybe what could be.

Believe.

He reached out a hand to help her across. As she stepped by Ozzie, Nancy and Josh, Alex squeezed her hand, ever so lightly. And when she slipped into the seat alongside him, he didn't let go. He just sat there, holding her hand, making her feel like the most desirable woman in the world with that simple touch, a gesture others would notice, for sure.

And regardless of what happened at the doctor's office, it felt good.

Chapter Sixteen

"Lisa, good morning." Dr. Alvarez shook Lisa's hand, indicated the seat across from her and opened Lisa's folder as Lisa sat down. "Let's cut right to the chase: there is no cancer."

Relief washed over Lisa, as if the sun just broke through a rain-soaked morning. "You're sure?"

Dr. Alvarez nodded. "The tests found nothing of note. What you do have are some fibroid tumors thickening the lining of the uterus. They're benign, they can be uncomfortable, and they're probably there because your hormones are in a jumble from the medicines, but for the moment we can just watch and see. Simply put, they're a thickening of the muscle tissue of the uterus. Once you're off the chemo, the hormones may adjust to a normal level and they could disappear entirely on their own. Nothing to worry about. Fibroids are quite common in women as they age. Your chemo has fooled your body into thinking you're older than you are. Once you're done with it in…" she eyed the chart "…two months, things may go back to whatever should be normal for you now."

"And that's it?"

The doctor smiled. "That's it."

All that worry for nothing. She'd read the stats, she knew what fibroids were, she understood that possibility, but she'd sailed over that info and zeroed in on the cancer risk.

She stood.

So did the doctor.

"Thank you, Doctor. I feel silly."

Dr. Alvarez shot her a look of amazement as they moved to the office door. "You shouldn't. I'd rather have patients come in and be checked before things get out of hand, than after. God gave you one body, Lisa. One vessel. It's okay to take care of it."

"You're right." Lisa paused at the door as she turned to say goodbye. "But I need to stop seeing cancer's shadow everywhere I go. In everything I do. It's time to trust that it's gone, once and for all."

"On a personal level, yes. But the whole Southern Tier appreciates all you're doing to heighten awareness, Lisa. As long as it doesn't impinge on your mental health."

It wouldn't if Lisa guarded against it better, spiritually and emotionally. She reached out and gave the doctor a quick hug. "Thank you."

Dr. Alvarez smiled and tapped the chart in her hand. "You're welcome."

* * *

"Dad?" Emma perked up as Alex pulled into the parking lot adjacent to a long white single-story building on Friday morning. "Why are we here?"

"Where's here?" Becky popped her head up from the game system in front of her. Her gaze wandered, suspicious, then hopeful as she read the Hornell Animal Shelter sign. "Dad, are we—?"

"Getting a dog?" Emma finished the question, eyes wide.

"I've been wanting a dog forever!" Josh declared.

Alex swiveled to face the girls. Always eager to be unleashed, Josh hung over the seat, eyes wide. "Back when Mommy was sick and you guys were small and I was going a little crazy, I gave your puppy to some nice people up near Rochester."

Emma nodded.

Becky did, too, but then she reached out a hand to his cheek, his face. "You had to, Dad. We weren't being much help with him."

Bless her heart. She was five years old at the time, her mother dying, she was in her first year of school and she felt guilty because she hadn't helped enough with the overgrown pup they'd adopted when Jenny was doing well. "It wasn't your fault, Becks. Or Emma's. It wasn't really anyone's fault, except maybe mine, but sometimes even grown-ups get overwhelmed."

Emma nodded. "I know, Dad."

"So." He jutted his chin toward the shelter door.

"I called these folks yesterday. They have some nice dogs here and I thought we'd stop by now that you guys are out of school for the summer and see about getting a dog. If you'd still like one, that is."

"We do!" Josh made the declaration at the top of his lungs.

"Dad." Becky leaned close as if concerned for Josh's feelings. "We don't have enough money. Emma and I only have twelve-fifty between us."

"I'm paying." He met both of their looks with a firm but happy one of his own. "It's the least I can do. If we find one we want."

"How will we know which one needs us the most?" Emma asked.

"The eyes," Becky declared. "You can always tell by the eyes. Miss Viola told Lisa yesterday that she could tell something was wrong by her eyes, so that's where we should look first."

"The eyes." Emma nodded and shrugged. "That kind of makes sense."

Alex zeroed in on Becky's revelation. "You overheard Miss Viola and Lisa talking?"

Becky nodded, anxious to climb out of the car. "Yes. But I wasn't eavesdropping, Dad." She gave him her classic eye roll. "Lisa was late and I wanted to help her get class started. That's when I heard her say she was going to see the doctor this morning because he did some tests."

Alex didn't doubt the veracity of the eight-year-old's words because Becky had spent years hearing about tests, scans and checkups. But why would Lisa's doctor order tests?

"Did she mention the doctor's name?" He asked the question with more nonchalance than he felt.

Becky frowned, thinking, then snapped her fingers. "Dr. Elvis. In Olean."

Alex pulled out his smart phone and did a quick scan of the phrase "Oncologist Olean, New York." The second name on the list jumped out at him: Dr. Emily Alvarez, gynecological oncology.

Alex switched his attention to meet his children's uplifted gazes. Three kids, three gifts, three little beings brought into the world by a mother who loved them. Loved him.

But Jenny was gone. Nothing could bring her back. And Lisa was here, right now. And she needed him. Needed them. He leaned closer and held their attention with his look and his voice. "Guys. There's something we need to do right now. And as soon as we're done, we'll come back here and pick out a dog, okay? But we would be wrong to make this decision without Lisa here. She needs to be with us."

"Oh, I like Lisa!" Josh fist-pumped the air and scrambled back into his seat.

Emma reached out a hand to Alex's arm. "That's a good idea, Dad. We should have thought of that sooner."

She was right, but he'd been assuming he had time. What if the unthinkable happened? What if they didn't have time?

It didn't matter, he decided. Letting Lisa face a crucial moment alone didn't make the short list. He started to turn the car around, then paused and caught Becky's gaze in the rearview mirror. "You okay with this, Beck?"

"Is she sick again, Daddy?"

"I hope not, honey. But if she is, she'll need friends, right?"

"Yes." Becky sank into her seat, adjusted her shoulder harness and waved toward the road. "Sitting here's getting us nowhere, Dad."

She was right. He called the garden center, just in case Lisa was there. She wasn't, and when he pressed Caro about the doctor visit Becky overheard, she admitted that Lisa was in Olean now. Right now.

He aimed west on I-86, and parked outside the professional building listed on the internet website. He jumped out of the car, corralled the kids, herded them to the curb, up the stairs and ushered them into a quiet waiting room.

A dear and familiar woman stood at the reception desk, her back to them. Their not-so-quiet entry made her turn. Surprise brought quick emotion to her eyes. She sought his gaze and a look of wonder joined the tears. "Alex?"

"Are you okay?"

She frowned. Her expression softened as understanding dawned. "Yes. Nothing major at all. But how did you…?" She saw Becky's look and nodded. "Someone overheard me talking to Viola yesterday."

"But I wasn't really listening!" Becky raced forward, grabbed Lisa in a hug and gazed up, imploring. "I just heard a few words and Daddy said that no matter what was going on, you'd need us around. Was he right, Lisa?" She leaned back and peered up, her little-girl look beseeching. "Do you need us?"

"I do." Lisa said the words simply, grazed a hand to Becky's cheek, then raised her eyes to Emma, Alex and Josh. "I need every single one of you. Every day. What do you think about that?"

"Wonderful?" Emma breathed the one-word response from her father's arm, grinning.

Alex crossed the room, intent, his gaze assessing. "So what did she say? Why are you here? And why didn't you tell me, Lisa?"

"Three absolutely marvelous reasons." She settled a look on each child in turn. "But it turns out that once again I was borrowing trouble, worried about nothing, and I should know better, Alex Steele, because I've done it before and it's utterly ridiculous."

He leaned in and brushed the sweetest, gentlest of kisses across her mouth, her cheek. "Not ridiculous at all. But next time, you'll tell me and we can both watch and worry for a few weeks, okay?"

"Really?" She passed a soft hand to Josh's face, marveling at the silky-sweet smoothness of the little boy. "Because I hated carrying this burden alone."

"Never again, Lisa." Alex reached out, hauled her into his free arm and hugged her tightly. "From now on we're in this together. You. Me. Them." He swept the kids a look that said they'd be along for the ride. "Oh. And the dog."

"The what?"

"Our dog," Josh explained. "Daddy said we couldn't pick out the dog without you so we drove all this way but the place might close so can we hurry, please? Because I've been wanting to get a dog all my life."

Lisa burst out laughing. She bent, gathered Josh up, grasped Emma's hand and smiled at Becky. "You did good, kid."

Becky grinned, smug. "I know."

"You're all set here?" Alex asked as he noted the women behind the desk watching them. Bright smiles of combined approval met his gaze.

"Yes." Lisa turned and waved. "See you next year, ladies. For my regular checkup."

"We'll be here, Lisa."

She went through the door with Josh and Emma in tow, and when Alex reached ahead to open the heavier outside door, it was a natural move to turn and find his mouth with hers. Kiss him, gently, lightly, right here with the children around. "Thank you."

He smiled, touched a finger to the tip of her nose, then followed the finger with a soft kiss. "For?"

"Finding me. Coming after me."

"Loving you."

Her eyes grew moist, but he thwarted the tears with a quick look at his phone. "We've got an hour before the shelter closes today. Think we can make it without getting a ticket?"

Lisa settled Josh into his seat, buckled his straps and aimed a look at Alex. "If not, I know a cop who might put in a good word for us."

"Is he a good cop?" he wondered out loud and smiled when Lisa laid her hand atop his.

"He's the best."

They made it with twenty minutes to spare. Josh held Alex's hand. He'd made a brave showing of wanting a dog, but when the chorus of barking sounded as they entered the kennel area, he shrunk against his father's leg.

They walked down the row, reading the cards on each dog's kennel. As the girls began to discuss the situation back and forth, Alex wondered if he'd have been smarter to come alone. Or bring one kid. But then, which one?

"Emma, I think you're right." Becky uttered the phrase in such a grown-up, agreeable tone that Alex stopped in his tracks. He didn't dare make eye contact because he might make a smart aleck remark and ruin the moment. He gripped Lisa's hand, slid his eyes to the right and watched as she recognized the sweet interaction.

She smiled, paused and listened along with him.

"I've looked at each one's eyes, and this guy seems to be saying something to me, Dad."

"Me, too." Emma reached in to pet the red-gold shaggy fellow. His soft green eyes brightened as the girls stroked the mutt's silky head. "It says he's almost two years old."

"And his owner had to move," added Becky.

"And he's got curly hair like Lisa," noted Josh, not to be outdone. "It's really soft, too."

"His name is Charley."

"And that's a really good name for a dog, I think." Josh's firm nod said the whole thing was all right by him.

The attendant opened the cage, attached a lead to the dog's collar and led them to the walking area. "Take a little time to get to know him. I don't mind staying extra."

"You're sure?" Alex turned, surprised. "We don't mean to keep you late."

"If he finds a good home, it's well worth it," she assured him. "I'll be inside, straightening up."

Inside, the dog had seemed docile. Quiet. Almost too quiet, making Alex wonder what was wrong. Outside?

Charley came alive, running with the kids. He didn't nip, bite or jump on them, a huge plus. And when Lisa sat down on the ground and let the dog slobber all over her with quick kisses and happy yips, Alex knew they'd found a keeper.

"So, what do you guys think? Should Charley come home with us?"

Becky laughed out loud. "Dad, we couldn't possibly leave him behind now. Not when we've gotten his hopes up. That would be so wrong!"

In this case she was right. Alex left them to play with the dog while he went inside to settle things. He'd gone shopping the day before. Everything Charley needed was tucked in the back of the SUV, out of sight. When he went back outside, papers in hand, the beauty of the visual made him stop.

Lisa. Emma. Becky. Josh. All smiling, all happy. And the dog, leaping for a Frisbee they'd found somewhere. Snagging the disc, mid-air, like that movie dog kids loved to watch.

It fit. They fit. The dog fit.

He pulled in a breath that had stopped hurting weeks ago, a breath that seemed fresh and new. Uncluttered. Unsullied.

And then he went to gather up his new family. His new normal.

Epilogue

"Emma? Have you got the shirts?"

"Right here." She chased down the stairs, lofted two plastic-wrapped T-shirts across the living room, then dashed back up. "Gotta brush my teeth."

"Hurry."

A slight pause ensued, followed by, "Dad! Charley ate my toothbrush!"

Alex didn't miss a beat. "The whole thing?"

"Naw. Just the end."

"Get a new one out of the medicine cabinet and I'll corral the dog."

"Okay!"

"Becky. Here's your shirt." Alex peeled the plastic from one pink T-shirt and set it beside Becky's half-full cereal bowl. "Drink the milk."

"Do I have to?"

"Yes. Next time don't use so much. Where's your brother?"

He found Josh standing on his head in the family room. He opened the second T-shirt, flipped the boy right side up and tugged the shirt over his head. "You've got a big head, kid."

"Because I've got so many brains in there." Josh peered at the shirt, upside down. "It's got Lisa's ribbon on it."

"It does. Em. You ready?"

"Yup." She raced down the stairs, grabbed a pink leash and laughed at her father's wince. "Dad. Get over it. He's color-blind."

"But smart," Alex countered. "He can probably sense the pinkness of that leash."

"I think he looks just marvelous," Becky crowed. "And it matches his pink collar, Dad."

"He's an awareness dog," Emma crooned, close to Charley's face. "He's doing his part for the cause."

He was, Alex decided. Like the rest of the family.

"And he smells like toothpaste," Josh added. He hugged Charley and pulled on his sandals. "Are we ready to go?"

"Let's do it." Alex put the supplies he'd need for the day into the back of the SUV with the dog, despite Josh's earnest plea to ride in the back so Charley could have his seat. "Don't eat this," he instructed the animal. He started to close the hatch, then eyed the dog.

Cute. Hairy. Red. And he'd already eaten one sneaker and now a toothbrush.

Alex reconsidered, gave Charley a short whistle

and brought him into the front seat with him. Better safe than sorry.

They pulled up to the high school parking lot shortly after nine. Floats, marching bands, fire trucks and civic groups milled around the school grounds. From below, it was hard to pick out any one group or float, so Alex took the grass route up the hill and parked.

A blast of pink stood out from the sea of red, white and blue bunting.

He corralled the kids, handed Emma the leash, then opened the back hatch again. He pulled out his own personal banner and looped it around shoulder and waist.

Emma laughed, delighted.

Becky grinned and high-fived him.

Josh peered up. "L-I-S-A..." he spelled, slowly. "Lisa!"

"Good job, bud!" Alex lifted him up and hugged him. "You read that all by yourself."

"I know. My teacher says I'm stinkin' smart."

"And she's correct." Alex grabbed the dog's leash and met the girls' gazes. "Are we ready?"

Emma's nod said she read beneath the surface of his question. She thinned her lips, then smiled. Nodded. "Yes."

"Beck?"

"We're getting nothing done standing here, Dad."

"That's my girl." He grinned down, tweaked her pink baseball cap and started forward. "Let's go."

They moved through the throngs of people. Few noticed them at first, but as more and more people read Alex's banner, talk shimmered from group to group. By the time they drew close to the breast cancer awareness float, folks were watching and waiting, all around.

Today, he and his family were the talk of the town. The center of attention. And if all went well in a few moments, he wouldn't mind in the least. He slipped the banner off as they approached the Breast Cancer Corps float, wanting to surprise Lisa. Make her day. And if she answered the printed question with a "yes"? She'd make his day, too.

"The bunting is perfect, Vi. I love it."

"Me, too. And those balloon ribbons?" Viola pointed to the four corners of the float where Ozzie's breast cancer balloon ribbons marked their mission. "Amazing."

"Lisa, here's a lei."

"Love it!" she declared, draping the pink floral necklace around her shoulders. "We've got the music ready, right?"

"Right here." Sabrina double-checked the CD of uplifting tunes and did a sound check. "The speakers appear to be working fine," she added when the quick noise startled a group of square dancers standing nearby. She raised her gaze to Lisa's, then paused, grinning, looking somewhere beyond Lisa's left shoulder. "We've got company."

"Do we? Awesome." Lisa turned, not sure what to expect, but when she saw Alex, three kids and a dog, all decked out to march with their float, tears smarted her eyes.

Pink baseball caps with the breast cancer ribbon covered each of their heads.

The three kids were wearing T-shirts that said "I wear pink for my Mom," and that only made her eyes water more.

Alex's shirt declared that he wore pink for his wife, and Lisa's heart melted further, glad he'd come to a great level of peace with Jenny's death.

But then Alex paused before the float. He pulled out a long white banner that had been draped over his shoulder. Silent, he watched her as he put it on, his gaze saying he'd taken on her battle wholeheartedly. The banner was done in a plain bold pink font and read simply: "Lisa, will you marry me/us?"

The import of his shirt and his question hit her full force.

He wanted her. They wanted her. Even the dog got into the act by pawing the wheel of the float as Alex dropped to one knee in front of everyone.

Quick tears streamed down Lisa's face.

Alex proffered a ring and a raised brow.

She nodded.

He grinned, stood and held out his arms.

She jumped off the float, into his embrace, a hug she wanted to enjoy forever.

Laughter and clapping surround-sounded them,

a sweet backdrop for the eager embraces of three children, a dog and a man who loved her, just as she was.

Lisa didn't need fireworks or pomp and pageantry to tell her today was special. She had everything she needed right here, in Alex's arms.

* * * * *

If you enjoyed this book by Ruth Logan Herne,
be sure to check out her next story
set in Kirkwood Lake, coming in September
from Love Inspired Books!

Dear Reader,

On June 17, 2011, my thirty-six-year-old friend Lisa was diagnosed with breast cancer. She is a special education teacher, married to a great guy and has four children under age eleven. Her youngest child was fifteen months old at the time. There is no history of breast cancer in her family. She exercised, ate right and still got cancer.

First, we cried. Then we fought. Lisa underwent a mastectomy, reconstructive surgery, two rounds of chemo and weeks of radiation. Her ongoing fight has been an inspiration to many. We are blessed to know and love her and her delightful family.

With Lisa's permission, I fashioned a breast cancer story to honor her and others who've waged war against this disease. While the war is won more often these days, breast cancer still presents a grim diagnosis and a sketchy prognosis. We don't look at odds and statistics anymore. Now, we pray. We laugh. We celebrate each milestone of her recovery. We employ humor, we embrace faith, we believe in God's everlasting love on both sides of heaven. We take great delight in whatever time He gives us.

Cancer hits most families at one time or another. And getting through the treatments is a rugged walk. Please join me in a heartfelt prayer that with God's help, science can unlock the key to shutting cancer down. If you want to talk more about this or just visit me, come see me at my blog, www.ruthys-place.com, email me at ruthy@ruthloganherne.com, visit me in Seekerville at www.seekerville.blogspot.com or visit me on the web at www.ruthloganherne.com. You can always snail mail me in care of Love Inspired Books, 233 Broadway, Suite 1001, New York, NY 10279. I love chatting with readers and I thank you for taking the time to make my work part of your life.

Asking God to bless you with life to the full...

Ruthy

Questions for Discussion

1. Losing his wife turned Alex Steele's life upside down in many ways. He lost his beloved; his children lost their mother. When do parents get time to truly grieve when they have children depending on them? And what could we do to help someone in that situation?

2. Alex decides to move the entire family to a new venue, a new start. This is an effective move for grown-ups sometimes. Why doesn't it necessarily work as well for children?

3. Lisa has always been a faith-filled woman, but her faith has been undermined by the flurry of traumas that have shaken her to the core. She wonders if there is a God, and if so, what has He done for her lately? Have you ever felt like that?

4. Alex comes into Gardens & Greens determined to help Emma with her 4-H project, but the breast cancer awareness campaign throws him off-kilter. What would you do when faced with a situation you'd rather distance yourself from?

5. Although God assures us of His presence, we often feel alone in our struggles. The idea of

"letting go and letting God" is easier said than done. How can we connect better with the simple faith of a child when grown-up knowledge challenges that faith?

6. Lisa feels she must resist this attraction to Alex because her fight against breast cancer has left her scarred, emotional and uncertain of her fate. At what point do we get to take chances and live life to the full again?

7. Alex's relationship with his mother-in-law is shaky. He's determined to do things his way. Why is it easier to accept advice from a stranger than someone we love?

8. Lisa's strong, stoic personality pushes her to hide her fear. She loves helping others but is slow to seek help for herself. Why is asking for help for ourselves so much more difficult than helping others?

9. Emma is writing conversational letters to her late mother. Becky is pretending her mother is still alive. Josh is trying to solicit a new girlfriend for his dad so he can have a mother like everyone else. How can we help the children around us who've suffered from divorce, death, illness, abandonment?

10. Lisa isn't content with conquering her personal fight with cancer—she wants and needs to help others. This flies in the face of Alex's desire to put cancer behind him permanently. Have you ever been faced with something so difficult you just wanted to turn your back on it? Walk away?

11. I had an elderly friend Rose who became a widow during World War II. She never remarried because she worried about a new husband's effect on her young children. What advice would you give to a new couple with children from a former relationship? How would you advise them to ease a path into those children's lives?

LARGER-PRINT BOOKS!

GET 2 FREE LARGER-PRINT NOVELS PLUS 2 FREE MYSTERY GIFTS

Love Inspired

Larger-print novels are now available...

LARGER-PRINT BOOKS!

GET 2 FREE
LARGER-PRINT NOVELS
PLUS 2 FREE
MYSTERY GIFTS

Love Inspired®
SUSPENSE
RIVETING INSPIRATIONAL ROMANCE

Larger-print novels are now available...

LISLPDIR13R

ReaderService.com

Manage your account online!

- Review your order history
- Manage your payments
- Update your address

We've designed the Harlequin® Reader Service website just for you.

Enjoy all the features!

- Reader excerpts from any series
- Respond to mailings and special monthly offers
- Discover new series available to you
- Browse the Bonus Bucks catalog
- Share your feedback

Visit us at:

ReaderService.com